With the eyes of the townspeople on them,
the little twins pushed the switch

The Bobbsey Twins' Wonderful Winter Secret

By

LAURA LEE HOPE

GROSSET & DUNLAP

Publishers   *New York*

PRINTED IN THE UNITED STATES OF AMERICA

The Bobbsey Twins' Wonderful Winter Secret

CONTENTS

THE BOBBSEY TWINS'
WONDERFUL WINTER SECRET

CHAPTER I

A SPECIAL PRIZE

"HURRY, Flossie!" six-year-old Freddie Bobbsey called to his blond, blue-eyed twin. "We'll be late for school!"

Upstairs, Flossie, her cheeks pink with excitement, was rummaging through her closet. "I *know* it was here last night," she muttered.

Just then a slender, dark-haired girl appeared in the bedroom doorway. "What's the matter, honey?" she asked. "Have you lost something?"

"Yes, Nan," her chubby little sister replied. "I can't find my red snow cap. And I need it, 'cause it's snowing extra hard outside."

Nan walked into the room. "Did you look on the floor? Perhaps it fell off the hook."

She knelt down and together the girls searched the closet floor. The cap was not there.

"What sort of game are you two playing?" The words made Nan and Flossie turn on their

1

knees. There, grinning down at them, stood twelve-year-old Bert Bobbsey, who was Nan's twin.

"Flossie lost her snow cap," Nan explained, "and I'm helping her find it."

Bert grinned. "Well, I don't like to tell tales, but I saw Snap going downstairs a few minutes ago with something red in his mouth!"

Snap was the Bobbseys' shaggy white dog. The four children loved him, even though he was a great tease.

"Oh dear!" Flossie wailed. "Snap'll chew my cap up!" She ran to the head of the stairs. "Freddie!" she called. "Is Snap down there and does he have my cap?"

"I'll look, Sis," Freddie answered.

At that moment something white flashed past the bottom of the stairs. "Snap!" Flossie screamed. "Catch him, Freddie!"

The chase began. Snap, holding the red, furry cap in his teeth, ran wildly through the living room, the sun porch, and the dining room with Freddie racing after him. Suddenly the dog went under the dining table. There he crouched, his tail beating a tattoo on the floor while his eyes snapped with excitement.

The twins' father, a tall, handsome man with a quick smile, was having breakfast. "Snap giving you trouble?" he teased, as Freddie ran into the room. "Can't my little fat fireman catch him?"

Mr. Bobbsey called his younger son by this nickname because ever since Freddie could walk, he had insisted he was going to be a fireman when he grew up. Right now a toy fire engine was his favorite plaything.

"Snap has Flossie's snow cap," Freddie explained. He got down on his hands and knees and began to crawl under the table.

This delighted Snap. He gave a bounce and bolted from under the table toward the swinging door into the kitchen. At that moment the door opened and a jolly-looking colored woman came in carrying a platter of small sausages.

Crash! Snap ran squarely into Dinah. The plate fell to the floor! The dog, sniffing the fragrant aroma of the meat, dropped the cap and began to gobble up the sausages.

"It's all right, Dinah," Mr. Bobbsey said. His eyes twinkled as he watched Snap. "The dog enjoys your cooking, too."

Dinah Johnson helped with the housework at the Bobbseys'. She and her husband Sam lived on the third floor of the Bobbseys' comfortable, rambling house in Lakeport. Sam drove a truck at Mr. Bobbsey's lumberyard on Lake Metoka.

"I'm sorry, Mr. Bobbsey," Dinah apologized.

"Anyway, Dinah," Freddie spoke up, "you

made him drop Flossie's snow cap. Now we can get to school on time."

By this time Flossie and the older twins had run into the dining room, followed by their slim, pretty mother.

"What's going on here?" Mrs. Bobbsey asked, smiling pleasantly.

"Well, it seems Snap wanted Flossie's cap," Mr. Bobbsey said, chuckling, "but he settled for my sausages!"

Mrs. Bobbsey laughed. Then she said, "Dinah will get you some more, Richard."

"Yes ma'am, Mrs. Bobbsey. Right away!" the good-natured cook agreed.

Mrs. Bobbsey turned to the children. "It's getting late," she said. "You'd better hurry to school."

"We mustn't be late—especially this morning," Nan remarked. "We have Assembly first and there's going to be a special announcement."

In a few seconds the four children were on their way, bundled in heavy wraps. The drifts were over three feet high in some spots.

"This is great!" Bert exclaimed as he stopped to scoop up a handful of snow and toss it playfully at Freddie.

"I love snow!" Nan cried, turning her face toward the drifting flakes. "It makes me think of winter sports, and Christmas!"

"When is Christmas, Nan?" Flossie asked, skipping along beside her sister.

"Just two weeks from today," Nan replied.

"By the way, what are we going to do about Mother's and Dad's gifts? I think it would be nice if we all chipped in and gave them something together."

"That's a good idea," Bert agreed. "But what?"

"Maybe they'd like a new garden hose," Freddie suggested.

Bert grinned at his little brother. "You wouldn't be planning to use it, would you?" he teased.

Freddie looked embarrassed. "Well, it would be good in case of a fire," he replied.

"I know!" Flossie cried. "Let's give them a baby kitten!"

Nan laughed. "We have a cat—Snoop. And after this morning, I don't think Dad will want any more pets! Anyway, I think Mother and Dad would like something which the four of us could make."

"Oh yes, that would be fun!" Flossie agreed. "What can we do?"

By this time the children were approaching the modern school building. The playground at the side was filled with boys and girls playing in the fresh, clean snow.

"Let's all think about what to make and talk it over tonight," Bert suggested. He suddenly saw his best friend, Charlie Mason, and ran to join the good-looking, brown-eyed boy.

Freddie and Flossie hurried into the building. They were very fond of their teacher, Miss Burns.

Meanwhile, a blond, pretty girl came up and linked her arm through Nan's. She was Nellie Parks, who often joined the Bobbsey twins in their adventures.

"Hi, Nellie!" Nan said. "Aren't you excited about Assembly this morning?"

"You mean about the fall achievement prizes being given out?" Nellie replied as the two girls fell into step and walked toward the school door. "I'm counting on you to get one of them, Nan!"

"Don't count too hard," Nan said. "The competition is terrific." At this moment the first bell rang and the girls hurried to their classroom, where attendance was taken.

When the second bell sounded the children filed out into the hall and joined others on their way to the auditorium. Bert and Charlie walked together.

"Are you nervous, Charlie?" Bert asked teasingly.

Charlie grinned. "No reason for me to be nervous. I'm not going to win anything!"

"That makes two of us then," Bert said, grinning.

When all the children were in their places, Mr. Tetlow, the principal, walked out onto the stage. He was a slender, gray-haired man and very popular with the students at Lakeport School.

After the regular Assembly program was over, Mr. Tetlow cleared his throat and said, "Today I shall award prizes for improvement and achievement in schoolwork during the fall term. As I call the names, the boy or girl will please come to the stage to receive the prize."

The principal began to read. The first children named received medals and citations for attendance, promptness, and conduct. Next would come the prizes in the various subjects studied. There was a ripple of excitement over the big room as Mr. Tetlow picked up his list.

"I'm all pins and needles!" Nellie whispered to Nan.

"To Bert Bobbsey," Mr. Tetlow announced, "a new atlas for the best map drawn in Geography class."

Bert looked surprised but pleased, as he made his way to the stage to receive his prize. There was a generous burst of applause from the children in the audience.

"To Nellie Parks a French dictionary for her excellent work in that language."

Nan threw her arms around her friend. "Oh, I'm so glad!" she cried.

When Nellie had returned from the platform with her award, Mr. Tetlow cleared his throat and announced with a twinkle in his eyes:

"I am particularly pleased to give this award. It goes to Charlie Mason for the greatest improvement in Arithmetic!"

Everyone clapped as Charlie, his face red with embarrassment and delight, went to the stage. Mr. Tetlow shook the boy's hand and presented him with a hockey stick.

"The last prize is the award for the best original play written in Miss Moore's English class."

Silence settled over the auditorium. This was the most important award of all the fall prizes.

Smilingly Mr. Tetlow picked up a pair of beautiful white figure skates. "These go to the writer of that play—"

There was an excited murmur from the audience. Who was the winner?

CHAPTER II

A CHRISTMAS SECRET

AS EVERYONE grew quiet again and waited for the announcement of the award winner for the best play, Mr. Tetlow stepped to the edge of the platform.

"Will Nan Bobbsey please come up to receive her prize?" he said, smiling.

A wave of applause swept the school auditorium as a blushing Nan made her way to the stage and thanked the principal. Then, clutching the ice skates, she walked back to her seat, a radiant smile on her face.

"Congratulations, Sis!" Bert whispered as she went past him. "I'm sure proud of you!"

"And I'm glad your map won the prize."

At noon when they started for home with Nellie and Charlie, Bert grinned.

"How about that French prize by Mademoiselle Nellie!"

"And Charlie a prize adder and subtracter!" said Nan. "I think we're all pretty lucky!"

As the four friends walked on together, they began to discuss the coming holidays.

"My dad read a long-range weather forecast," Charlie remarked. "It predicted lots of snow and cold weather coming up."

"Great!" Bert exclaimed. "We can have some keen times during vacation. I never get enough coasting and skiing!"

Nan held up her new skates. "Maybe if I practice with these, I can become really good!"

"I'll teach you to play hockey, Nan," Charlie offered, waving his new hockey stick.

Nellie looked at Bert. "I don't know how we can use our prizes outdoors, Bert, but you might use your atlas to show Nan some places where they have skating contests, so she can go and win a prize."

"Right." Bert entered into the game. "And you can translate the hockey rules into French for Charlie in case he ever plays in France."

At the next corner the four children lingered a minute before parting for their homes.

Suddenly Bert looked up the street and muttered, "Here comes trouble—Danny Rugg!"

"And with Jack Westley, of course!" Charlie added. "Everyone look out!"

Danny Rugg was the same age as Bert and Charlie, but taller and heavier. Jack Westley was his pal, and both boys were bullies. They took particular delight in playing tricks on the Bobbsey twins.

Now they strolled up to the other children with sneering looks on their faces. "Well, I see the Bobbseys are little tin heroes again," Danny said. "I heard Nan's play read in class, and boy, was that a bore!"

"They're just teachers' pets!" Jack joined in. "The Bobbseys probably entertained Mr. Tetlow at their home before the prizes were awarded."

"You're just jealous, Danny Rugg, because you didn't win a prize," Nellie said hotly.

"Is that so!" Danny jeered. "Well, I guess I'll take this prize!" With that he grabbed the skates from Nan's hand and ran off down the street.

When Bert recovered from his surprise, he started after the bully. But as he did so, Jack Westley stuck out his foot and Bert fell headlong into a snowbank!

Charlie stopped to help Bert onto his feet and by that time the two troublemakers were far away. As he ran, Danny tossed Nan's skates onto a snow-covered lawn.

Danny grabbed the skates from Nan's hands

"I'll get Danny for this!" Bert vowed between clenched teeth, as he brushed the cold
snow off his face and coat.

"Oh, don't worry about him, Bert," Nan said.
"You know Danny. His day wouldn't be com-
plete without at least one mean trick!"

Charlie waded through the snow and brought
back the skates. Nan thanked him, and she and
Bert turned toward home.

"Have you thought any more about Mother's
and Dad's Christmas gifts?" Bert asked.

"Yes, but I haven't come up with anything
yet," Nan replied. "Have you?"

Bert's eyes twinkled. "Yes, I have," he said
mysteriously.

"What is it? Tell me!"

As they walked home, Bert outlined his plan.
"Do you think it will work?" he asked.

"It's wonderful, Bert!" Nan cried. "But won't
it cost a lot of money?"

"That's the only part which worries me," her
brother admitted. "But maybe I can think of
some way that won't cost much, and the four of
us should be able to earn some money before
Christmas."

"Freddie and Flossie will love your idea,"
Nan exclaimed. "You know how they go for
things like that."

"Let's try to get them alone after lunch and tell them about it," Bert proposed.

But this did not prove to be easy to do. The small twins were eating their lunch by the time Bert and Nan reached home. Mrs. Bobbsey was with them and eager to hear the results of the morning's program. Freddie and Flossie had already told her Nan and Bert had won prizes.

"Oh, children," she cried, "I'm so proud of you! Your father couldn't get home this noon but I phoned and told him the big news as soon as I heard it. He sent you his congratulations!"

"We were both surprised," Nan said.

When the older twins had eaten lunch, Nan looked meaningfully at her little sister. "If you'll come upstairs, Flossie," she urged, "I'll fix your hair."

"That's very nice, Nan," Mrs. Bobbsey said kindly, "but I'll do it."

Nan cast a discouraged look toward Bert. He winked at his sister and turned to Freddie. "Come out in the hall, will you? I have something in my pocket for you."

"Thanks, Bert," the younger boy replied. "Wait, I'll finish my pudding first."

Bert sighed and glanced at Nan. She quickly spoke up. "If you'll wait for us, Freddie and Flossie, we'll walk back to school with you."

Flossie jumped down from her chair. "We can't. Miss Burns is going to read us a story so we have to hurry back."

Nan looked so woebegone that Mrs. Bobbsey laughed. "I'd guess that Bert and Nan have a secret to tell you young twins. Perhaps you'd better walk to school with them."

"Oh sure, Nan. We'll wait for you," Flossie promised excitedly. "We *love* secrets!"

On the way back to school, Nan said to Freddie and Flossie, "Do you remember this morning we were wondering what to do for Mother's and Dad's Christmas?"

"Oh yes," Flossie answered. "You have an idea?"

"Bert has. He'll tell you about it."

After Bert had finished describing his plan, Flossie clapped her hands. "Oh, I think that's just scrumptious!"

"Yes, let's do it!" Freddie agreed enthusiastically.

"It will cost money," Nan cautioned. "But we think we can earn enough to pay for it before Christmas."

"I have fifty cents I was saving for Mommy's and Daddy's present," Flossie announced.

"I have seventy-five cents!" Freddie said proudly.

Nan explained that she might be able to earn some money baby-sitting. Bert thought he could find some snow-shoveling jobs.

"Maybe Freddie and I can run errands," Flossie suggested.

"We'll think of something," Nan assured her, as they reached the school building and separated to go to their classrooms.

Later that afternoon Bert and Nan joined Charlie and Nellie and a group of other boys and girls at a hill in the park nearby. It was a favorite spot with the children of Lakeport.

"Hi, Bert!" called Dick Hatton, one of Charlie's and Bert's classmates. "Come on over and help us. We're going to try to make a snow-slide."

"Okay," Bert replied, "that sounds like fun."

The Bobbseys walked over to join their friends and soon were at work with half a dozen other boys and girls trampling a smooth path on the slope. One after the other, they scuffed along, packing the snow hard under their boots. Finally a wide runway took shape.

"Now we should put water on it so it'll freeze and be really slick," Bert suggested, tamping down the few remaining rough spots.

"Good idea," Charlie agreed. "I'll get some from the 'shack.'" This was the nickname the children had given a small refreshment stand run by an old man in the neighborhood. In the summer he sold ice cream and soft drinks, and in the winter tasty frankfurters and steaming hot chocolate.

In a few moments Charlie returned carrying a pail of water. "It won't take long to freeze today!" he exclaimed as he walked along the path the children had made, dribbling the water onto the snow.

He was right. Almost before he reached the lower end of the path, the water was frozen solid. It made a gleaming ribbon of ice down the slope of the hill. The others watched him, eagerly awaiting their turns.

"I'll go first," Dick suggested, "and show you how."

He stood at the top of the slope. Then, standing on his left foot, he gave a push with the right. Down he started! Knees bent like a skier's, he fairly flew down the hill! One by one, the other boys followed until there was a continous stream of young sliders whizzing along behind him.

"This is great!" Bert cried as he came panting back to the top of the slope again. "You girls ought to try it," he said to Nan and Nellie.

"I'm game if you are," Nan said, looking questioningly at her friend.

Nellie tossed her blond hair and gave a sigh. "I guess it's now or never," she said. "Just follow me!"

She stood poised at the top of the path, then with a push of her right foot she was off! Down the icy slope she flew, her eyes sparkling and her cheeks burning with excitement. The others cheered her on.

Nan took her position and shoved off. Down she whizzed!

Suddenly Bert, who was watching from the sidelines, cried out in alarm and started to run down alongside the slide. He had seen something red on the path ahead of Nan—Nellie's scarf had blown off!

If Nan hit it, she would surely have a nasty fall!

CHAPTER III

PROJECT SANTA CLAUS

NAN, bent forward, slid speedily down the icy slope. Apparently she did not see the scarf that lay in her path.

Bert knew he never could get there in time to pull it out of the way.

"Nan!" he screamed. "Jump over the scarf! Jump!"

Nan was only a few feet from the scarf. She looked up, and gave a leap, sailing over the red cloth. As Nan came down, she swayed dangerously. But in a second she had regained her balance and sped to the bottom of the hill.

Bert joined Nan and Nellie at the end of the slide. "Say, Sis, that was a great jump," Bert complimented his twin.

"I feel terrible about it," Nellie said. "I was going too fast ⬛top when my scarf blew off.

It would have been my fault if you'd been hurt, Nan."

"Oh, Nellie, you couldn't help it, and I'm all right," Nan said. "But I think I've had enough sliding for this afternoon. I'm going home. See you later, Bert!"

"I have to get home, too, Nan," Nellie said. "I'll walk along with you."

The two girls waved good-by to the other children and left the park. When Nan reached home, Dinah told her that Mrs. Bobbsey was out shopping. Freddie and Flossie had gone to Susie Larker's house to play. Susie was Flossie's best friend and lived just down the street from the Bobbseys.

"I'm going upstairs and start my homework," Nan said.

"Okay, honey child," the jolly cook replied. "I'll be down in the basement if you want me."

Nan was deep in some arithmetic problems when the front doorbell rang. She waited a minute to see if Dinah had answered it. But when the bell sounded again she ran downstairs and opened the door. Outside stood an elderly woman with carefully combed white hair and twinkling blue eyes.

"Aunt Sally Pry!" Nan exclaimed.

Mrs. Pry was not related to the Bobbseys but the twins called her aunt. They had known the lovely old lady a long time. She was quite deaf, but refused to wear a hearing aid. For this reason she was the cause of many funny misunderstandings.

"Won't you come in?" Nan invited.

"Begin? What should I begin?" the little old lady replied. "I came to see your mother."

"I said, 'Won't you come in?' " Nan repeated in a louder voice.

"Oh, of course, my dear," Aunt Sally answered, smiling apologetically. "You know I'm a little hard of hearing. You must excuse me."

Nan ushered the caller into the living room. "Won't you sit down, Aunt Sally? Mother isn't in but I think she'll be home soon."

"Tune? What did you say about a tune, Nan?"

"I'm sorry," Nan replied with a smile. "I said Mother would be home soon."

"I think I'll wait for her then," Aunt Sally decided. "I want to tell her about my Christmas project."

"We twins have a Christmas project, too," Nan volunteered. "We've been trying to think of ways to earn money."

"You're selling honey?" Aunt Sally said quickly. "I'd be glad to buy some."

"Oh no, Aunt Sally." Nan raised her voice. "We want to earn some money."

"That's what I'm doing," the elderly woman agreed. "I'm making candy to sell."

"You make wonderful candy, Aunt Sally. I know Mother will want to buy some."

Mrs. Pry looked thoughtful. "If I just had someone to help me," she mused, "I could make a lot more."

Nan was thoughtful a moment. An idea had just come to her. Maybe she could help Aunt Sally and also earn her own share of the Christmas present money!

"Perhaps I can help you make the candy," she told Aunt Sally.

"You think my new hat is dandy?" Aunt Sally said brightly. "Why, thank you, Nan."

"It's very nice," Nan agreed, "but I was talking about your candy. Do you think I could be your helper?"

"Well now, Nan, perhaps you could," Mrs. Pry said slowly. "I never thought of that, but I remember you make good candy yourself—especially fudge."

Without disclosing the exact nature of their project, Nan told Aunt Sally about the twins' *Project Santa Claus* and how eager they were to make some extra money.

"I could use you for an hour each afternoon," Aunt Sally said. "You would be a great help to me and I'll be glad to pay you."

"Oh, thank you, Aunt Sally. That will be

wonderful!" Nan said. "I can start tomorrow morning—it's Saturday."

At this moment Freddie and Flossie ran into the room, their cheeks glowing from the cold.

Seeing the visitor, they dashed across the floor and threw their arms around her neck. Aunt Sally was very popular with the younger twins.

"We've been coasting!" Flossie announced.

"Roasting?" Aunt Sally exclaimed. "How could you be warm in this weather?"

Freddie and Flossie giggled. "No!" Freddie shouted. "We've been riding on Susie's new sled."

Mrs. Pry laughed as she hugged the small twins. "You see your old Aunt Sally still gets mixed up!"

Nan quickly told Freddie and Flossie that she was going to work for Aunt Sally and help her make Christmas candies.

"That's fun, Nan!" Flossie exclaimed. "Could I help, too, do you s'pose?"

Aunt Sally thought for a moment. "Would you like to pack the candies into the boxes, Flossie? You'd have to be very careful not to break them."

Flossie clapped her hands. "Goody! I'll be 'stremely careful and make pretty boxes!"

Realizing that his sisters had found ways to earn extra money and that he had not, Freddie looked discouraged.

"Don't you have anything that boys can do,

Aunt Sally?" he asked woefully. "Could I maybe be a candy taster—to see that they're all made right?"

Aunt Sally laughed and rumpled his yellow hair. "Well, Freddie," she said, "we'll have to think of something sensible. How about delivering the orders here in your neighborhood?"

"Oh sure!" Freddie agreed. "I can use my new sled."

"We must keep this a secret," Nan cautioned.

Just then Mrs. Bobbsey came home and walked into the room. She greeted her caller affectionately. The children stayed a few minutes longer. Then, excusing themselves, they ran upstairs where they excitedly discussed their new jobs.

"Won't Bert be surprised when we tell him?" Flossie said with a giggle.

Unfortunately Bert arrived home just in time for dinner and the children had no chance to tell him of their success. Afterward, though, Mr. and Mrs. Bobbsey went out and the twins gathered around the dining table to play games.

"Guess what, Bert," Freddie began. "Nan and Flossie are going to help Aunt Sally Pry make candy and I'll deliver it on my sled!"

"When did all this happen?" Bert asked.

Nan explained about Mrs. Pry's visit and her

project of making candy for Christmas. "And before Mother came home," she added, "we all had jobs!"

"That's swell!" Bert praised them. "And I haven't been idle myself!"

"What have you been doing?" Nan asked.

"Well, when I left the park, I went all around the neighborhood. I have four families lined up. I'm to keep their walks clear of snow for the next two weeks. I can do some of it before school, so I'll still have time to work on our project.

"That's wonderful, Bert!" Nan exclaimed. "Now I'm sure our project will be a success. Only we'll need someone to get it in shape for us. Whom can we ask?"

"I've thought of that, too," Bert admitted. "Do you remember Dad's friend, Mr. Holman? He might help us."

"Mr. Holman?" Nan looked puzzled. Then her expression cleared. "Of course! That's the kind of work he does. He's so nice, I'm sure he'll say yes."

"Let's go over and see him at his office to-morrow morning."

"Yes, let's," Nan said, and the small twins agreed.

"I can hardly wait!" Flossie said eagerly.

The next morning at breakfast Mrs. Bobbsey told the twins, "I'd like to take you all downtown for some Christmas shopping this morning. Will you be ready in an hour?"

The children exchanged dismayed glances. There was silence. All the twins wondered what would happen to their planned visit. Finally Nan spoke up.

"That's nice, Mother, but may we go later?"

Mrs. Bobbsey looked puzzled. "I suppose so," she replied. "But why put it off? The shopping may take us some time and I have an engagement this afternoon."

Flossie came to her sister's rescue. With a big smile she said, "We can't go on account of *Project Santa Claus!*"

CHAPTER IV

A BROTHER'S JOKE

WHEN Flossie mentioned *Project Santa Claus,* Mrs. Bobbsey smiled. "I can wait until ten-thirty, if that will help you," she said. "Suppose we all meet in the car at that time, ready to go shopping."

Flossie hugged her mother. "Oh, you're so nice!" she exclaimed.

After making their beds and straightening up their room, Nan and Flossie hurried off to Aunt Sally Pry's home. She was already busy making candy.

Nan tied on a big white apron and got ready to help. Flossie set the little white boxes out on a table and began to line them with waxed paper.

In the meantime Bert and Freddie cleaned the walks around the Bobbsey home. When they had finished, Bert put the largest snow shovel over his shoulder.

"I'll do the other walks now, Freddie," he said. "Are you going to start your deliveries?"

The little boy shook his head. "There's nothing ready yet. Aunt Sally told me not to come until Monday."

At that moment Dinah's voice sounded from the back door. "Freddie! Have you fed Snoop and Snap?"

"Oh, I forgot," he said, and ran around the side of the house calling, "I'm coming, Dinah!"

While Freddie was busy getting dog food, cat food, and water, Bert went off to his shoveling jobs. But promptly at ten-thirty the twins met in the driveway where the station wagon was parked. In a few minutes Mrs. Bobbsey came out of the house, buttoning up her coat.

"All aboard for the Christmas Express!" she called, and they piled in.

In a short while she parked the station wagon in the community lot and they set out for Lakeport's largest department store.

Mrs. Bobbsey planned to buy gifts for some out-of-town relatives and the children were eager to help. They visited several departments and soon the long list had dwindled to a few special items.

"We'll gift-wrap these at home," Mrs. Bobbsey said, "then mail them."

"The one I like best is for our Cousin Dorothy," said Nan. "I think she'll have fun wearing those donkey bedroom slippers."

"And Cousin Harry," Bert added with a grin, "will have to stay up nights to figure out those brain-twisting puzzles we bought."

During this conversation Freddie and Flossie had been whispering to each other. They had set aside some money especially to buy gifts for Bert and Nan. This was a good time to spend it, they decided.

"Mommy," Flossie said, "Freddie and I have some special shopping to do. May we meet you later?"

"All right. Meet me at the jewelry counter. It's near the front door. Come there when you've finished your shopping."

Nan was eager to look at the pretty costume jewelry, but Bert preferred going to the book department.

"I want to see if they have any new books on camping," he said.

Hand in hand, Freddie and Flossie made their way along the aisles until they came to a counter covered with an assortment of inexpensive gifts. They began to look through the items.

"How much money do you have, Freddie?" his twin asked as she opened her little red purse.

In reply Freddie reached into his pocket and pulled out two quarters. "This is all," he said ruefully. "I meant to save more, but somehow I didn't!"

Flossie giggled. "I know what you mean," she said. "I have sixty cents. But if we put our money together, maybe we can buy something nicer. Okay?"

"You mean we'd give them each one thing from both of us?"

"Yes."

"We-ell," Freddie said doubtfully, "I guess so."

"How do you like this?" Flossie picked up a clear plastic box containing a pink brush and comb decorated with sparkles.

"Say! That's neat for Nan!" Freddie exclaimed. He eyed the set admiringly.

Flossie asked the salesgirl the price. "One dollar," was the reply.

"Oh dear," Flossie cried. "I'm afraid that's too much! That would take almost all our money and we'd have only a dime left for Bert's present!"

"How about this for fifty cents?" the young woman suggested. She held up a pale-blue leather change purse stamped with a design in gold.

"That's pretty!" the little girl exclaimed. "Let's get it, Freddie."

Her twin agreed and the salesgirl put the little purse in a gay Christmas box. "Is there something else you'd like?" she asked.

"Yes, we want something for our big brother," Freddie spoke up. "He's twelve years old."

"Is he interested in plane models? We're having a special on them this week for fifty-nine cents."

"What do you think, Freddie?" Flossie asked.

"That would be great! Let's see them!" the little boy replied eagerly.

The salesgirl took several boxes from the shelf and spread them out on the counter. There were models of little two-seaters, cargo planes, and giant jet passenger liners.

One especially caught Freddie's eye. It was a warplane that shot tiny rockets. When he picked it up the salesgirl said regretfully, "I'm sorry, but that one isn't in the special sale. It's a dollar and a half."

"I like this one," Flossie said, pointing to the jet liner. "Look at all the little windows along the side!"

"All right," Freddie agreed reluctantly.

After Flossie and Freddie had paid for their purchases, Flossie held up a penny. "Look!" she said triumphantly. "We can put this in Nan's purse—for luck!"

The small twins collected their packages, then decided to look around the toy department.

"Mother won't be ready yet," said Freddie confidently, "so we have time."

"We were going to buy something for Dinah and Sam, too," Flossie reminded him.

"How can we? We haven't any money left!"

Flossie sighed. "That's right. We'll have to wait until we get our next week's allowances."

Freddie made his way to the toy display and Flossie followed. First the twins looked at Santa Claus who sat on a throne placed on a platform. Small children were lined up waiting to tell him what they wanted for Christmas. The Bobbseys joined them. Of course Flossie wanted another doll, and Freddie another fire apparatus toy!

"You might go to the counter and look at them," Santa suggested, so the twins walked to the counter.

"See that big hook-and-ladder truck!" Freddie exclaimed excitedly. "Isn't that super? It would be perfect with my fire engine!"

"It's neat, Freddie," Flossie agreed.

While he was admiring the fire truck, Flossie's attention was attracted to a wonderful big doll on a nearby counter. It looked so much like a real little girl that several women and children had stopped to admire it.

The doll was dressed in a red-plaid pleated skirt and black-velvet jacket. She wore a black tam perched jauntily on her yellow curls.

"Isn't she bee-yoo-ti-ful!" Flossie put out her hand and gently touched the doll. Suddenly she was startled to hear a voice exclaim:

"Hello! How are you?"

Flossie jumped back so fast that she knocked another doll off the counter. Freddie ran up just in time to catch it, and quickly put it back with the other toys.

"I'm awf'ly sorry," Flossie explained to the saleswoman who had just come up, "but I thought that big doll spoke to me!"

"If you touched her hand, she did," the clerk replied with a pleasant smile. "This is our very newest doll, called Miss Melody. She has a little phonograph inside her and when you touch her hand, the record plays and she talks."

The woman touched the doll as Flossie had done and once more the phonograph voice came out, "Hello! How are you?"

"I wish I could have a doll like that for Christmas!" Flossie sighed.

"I'm hungry! Let's have lunch!" came the piping voice again.

Flossie looked amazed, and even the saleswoman acted startled.

"How many things can she say?" Flossie asked.

"Well, I didn't know she could say that!" the woman exclaimed.

At that moment they heard a chuckle and turned around. Behind them stood Mrs. Bobbsey and the older twins.

"Oh, Bert, that was you!" Flossie exclaimed accusingly, and her big brother grinned.

Mrs. Bobbsey smiled and put an arm around her little daughter. "You know how he loves to tease you," she said. "What were you and Freddie so interested in?"

"Come see this doll," Flossie urged. "She talks when you touch her hand!"

"And look at this swell hook-and-ladder!" Freddie broke in.

Mrs. Bobbsey admired the toys, then suggested that they have luncheon. She led the way to an elevator and they took it to the top floor. In front of them was an attractive restaurant. The children enjoyed sitting by a window and looking down on the crowds in the street below.

When they finished eating, Nan said hesitantly, "Mother, would you mind if we don't go home with you? We twins have another errand to do."

"Not at all," Mrs. Bobbsey agreed, smiling. "As a matter of fact, I have a little private shopping to do myself. I'll see you at home."

When the children reached the street, Bert said, "Follow me."

"Do you know where Mr. Holman's office is?" Nan asked her twin.

"No, but I can find it."

"Don't you think we should phone and ask if we may come to talk to him?" Nan suggested.

"That's a good idea. Let's go in this drugstore and I'll call," Bert replied.

The others waited while he shut himself into a phone booth. In a few minutes he came out, a smile on his face.

"Mr. Holman says he'll be glad to help us and that we can come up to his office right now and talk it over."

"Is it far?" Flossie asked.

"No, it's in the James Building, two blocks from here."

The children set off up the street and soon came to the building. They stopped to study the names on the directory in the lobby. As they were reading it, a deep voice behind them said:

"What are you doing here, Bobbsey twins?"

CHAPTER V

AN EAVESDROPPER

AT THE sound of the deep voice the twins spun around. There stood Mr. Bobbsey!

"W-why, hello, Dad," Nan said hesitantly.

"Hello. What are you children doing here?" Mr. Bobbsey repeated, smiling. "I thought you were going shopping with your mother."

"We were—er, we did," Bert sputtered. "We're on our way home."

"Yes," Flossie spoke up. "We stopped in here to get warm!"

"Oh, I see," their father replied. "Well, I'm sorry I can't drive you home, but I have an appointment farther down the street. I'll walk along with you."

The twins were in despair but, in order not to reveal any hint of their secret, followed Mr. Bobbsey out of the building. He set off along the street at a brisk pace in the direction from which the children had come. Finally he stopped.

"This is where I'll have to leave you," he said. "Tell your mother I'll be home as soon as I can." Then, with a quick wave, he was off.

Nan laughed. "Well, that was a close one! Now we'll have to walk all the way back to the James Building!"

This time when they reached the building the twins stepped immediately into the waiting elevator.

"Where is Mr. Holman's office?" Bert asked the operator, whose name tag said he was Dave Brown.

"Fourth floor. But they're closed on Saturday afternoon," the man replied.

Bert explained that he had telephoned Mr. Holman and been told to come up. Dave shrugged his shoulders and ran the elevator to the fourth floor.

Across the hall and to the right of the elevator a door stood open. Bert read the sign on the glass. "Mr. Holman's office," he said.

At this moment a short, stout man came from an inner room. "Hello there, Bobbsey twins!" he boomed. Then, with his blue eyes twinkling merrily, he went on, "What's all this mystery about? Tell me what you have in mind."

As he spoke he ushered the children into his private office, but left the door to the hall open a crack.

"My secretary's not here this afternoon," Mr. Holman explained. "I'm leaving the door open so I can hear if anyone comes into the outer office."

"What 'citing pictures, Mr. Holman!" Flossie exclaimed as she looked around the walls.

"Yes, this is work I've done for some of my other clients," Mr. Holman said with a smile. "But now tell me about your plans."

Bert and Nan took turns outlining their ideas for *Project Santa Claus.* "Hmm, umm," Mr. Holman nodded his head as he listened. "Well," he said when they finished, "I don't see why we can't manage that. Would you want to do it here?"

"We were wondering if we could do it all at school after hours," Nan said eagerly.

Mr. Holman thought a moment. Then he said, "I think that could be arranged."

"We haven't much money!" Freddie spoke up. "Will that matter?"

Mr. Bobbsey's friend threw back his head and gave a hearty laugh. "Well, usually that would matter quite a bit, young man," he said, "but in the case of the Bobbseys' *Project Santa Claus,* we'll make the price fit the pocketbook!"

"Oh, thank you, Mr. Holman!" Nan exclaimed. "We're all earning money and we'll pay you before Christmas!"

At that moment Mr. Holman held up his hand. "Excuse me a minute," he said. "I hear someone in the front office." He left the room but returned in a second with a puzzled look on his face.

"That's funny," he mused. "I was sure I heard someone out there. And I'm also positive I left the outside door open, but it's closed now!"

"Maybe someone did come in, but went away when he heard us talking," Bert suggested.

"You're probably right," Mr. Holman agreed. "Well now, let's get this project lined up."

For the next twenty minutes different problems were discussed and solved and tentative plans made. Finally Mr. Holman closed his notebook with a smile. "I think that about takes care of everything. You can let me know when you're ready to start."

"We will!" Nan exclaimed enthusiastically. "And thank you a million!"

Mr. Holman shook hands with all the twins, then they filed out into the hall. As the children walked toward the elevator they saw a familiar figure standing there. It was Danny Rugg!

"Hello, Danny," Bert said. "What are you doing here?"

"I guess I can come here if I want to!" the boy answered rudely. "My father's office is right over there!" He pointed across the hall. With a grin Danny said, "I know why you're here! It's a silly idea, too!"

"You're the one who came into Mr. Holman's office!" Freddie accused him.

"And you listened!" Flossie exclaimed angrily.

"I did not! I was going by the door and you were talking so loudly I couldn't help hearing! And I think I'll tell your mother and father what you're planning to do!"

"Oh, Danny! Please don't. We want it for a Christmas surprise!" Nan pleaded.

The bully shrugged his shoulders. "Well, I'll think about it," he said. "I may tell and I may not."

By this time the elevator had arrived and the children rode down in silence. At the building entrance they separated and the Bobbsey twins hurried home.

As they neared the house Nan said in a worried tone, "I hope Danny won't tell. Isn't it a shame that he found out about it."

"I'd like to fight him!" Freddie exclaimed, clenching his fists.

That night at supper the twins were still thinking about the bully and were more quiet than usual. When Dinah served a dessert of fruit custard, Mr. Bobbsey announced, "I heard some interesting news this afternoon at the meeting of the Town Council."

"What was it, Dick?" Mrs. Bobbsey asked.

"Since we have so much snow and it seems likely to continue until after Christmas, the

Council has decided to sponsor a snow-sculpture contest."

Flossie put down her spoon. "Daddy, what fun! Are we going to enter?"

"Would you like to, my fat fairy?" This was Mr. Bobbsey's favorite nickname for his small, chubby daughter.

Flossie nodded excitedly and the others bombarded their father with questions.

"When will it be?"

"What shall we make?"

"What is the prize?"

Mr. Bobbsey held up his hands in pretended dismay. "Wait a minute! One at a time!"

When the children were quiet again, their father began to explain. "The Council hopes many Lakeport residents will make a statue or other object out of snow in their front yards. On the afternoon of Christmas Eve the Council members will view the sculptures and decide which one is the best and most original. Then a cash prize will be awarded to the winner. Honorable mention will go to the second and third best."

"Say," Bert spoke up excitedly, "if all six of us worked on it, we could make something really keen!"

"Yes," Mrs. Bobbsey agreed. "It would be fun for the whole family to do. Could you come home early a few afternoons and help us, Richard?"

"I think that could be arranged," Mr. Bobbsey agreed.

"Oh, goody!" Flossie exclaimed. "What shall we make?"

All sorts of suggestions were offered. Freddie thought a figure of Santa Claus would be good. Bert was in favor of a reindeer. Flossie wanted to make a snow Christmas tree.

Finally Nan spoke up. "Don't you think we ought to try something harder? How about figures of Cinderella and Prince Charming?"

"That's a lovely idea, Nan," her mother agreed. "I'll vote for that!"

It was quickly decided to make the fairy-tale figures and Mr. Bobbsey promised to save time to help in the sculpturing.

The next day, after church and one of Dinah's special Sunday dinners, the twins met in the third-floor playroom to make further plans for their secret *Project Santa Claus.*

"The first thing to do," Bert announced, "is to make a list of the items we'll need." He got a pad and pencil from a table drawer and sat down. "All right," he said, "let's begin."

Everyone made suggestions and in a short while the pad was full. Bert stood up. "There are some old cartons in the garage we can use. I'll get them."

He dashed downstairs, hurriedly pulled on a coat, and ran to the garage. When he opened the door, there was Sam Johnson polishing the station wagon.

Bert was taken aback, but said, "Hello, Sam. I came for a few of these cartons."

Sam, who was usually smiling, frowned slightly. "I was fixin' to save those."

"Oh, come on, Sam," Bert pleaded. "You don't want all these. Nan and Freddie and Flossie and I need some for a project we're working on."

"We-ell," Sam hesitated, "I guess maybe I can spare three."

"Okay. Thanks, Sam." Bert hurriedly gathered up the cartons and ran from the garage. "Whew!" he exclaimed when he got back to the playroom. "Sam almost didn't let me have these!"

Flossie whispered to Nan. "There's an old mop handle in the basement. It would be perfect. I'll go get it."

The little girl skipped downstairs. The kitchen was empty when she reached it. She tiptoed quietly down the basement steps. The fruit closet was at the bottom and Dinah stood there inspecting some jelly glasses.

As Flossie passed behind her the cook jumped. The glass in her hand crashed to the concrete floor and shattered. "Land alive!" Dinah exclaimed. "What are you doin' tiptoein' around down here like that, Flossie? You sure scared me!"

Flossie giggled. "I'm sorry, Dinah, I didn't mean to. I just came to get something. I'll clean up the glass."

"Never mind, honey child. I'll do it." Dinah lumbered up the steps to get a dustpan and broom.

Flossie went into the laundry. "I'd better find that mop handle and get upstairs before Dinah starts asking any more questions," she told herself with a giggle.

But it took Flossie longer than she thought and she met Dinah coming down to the basement again. "What's that, Flossie?" the cook asked suspiciously.

"It's just an old mop handle," the little girl replied. "Please let me take it, Dinah. We need it for a Christmas surprise."

"Now what kind of Christmas surprise would an old mop make?" Dinah asked, chuckling.

"You'll find out later!" Flossie cried and ran up to the kitchen.

Dinah shook her head and went back to her sweeping. The next moment she heard a scream and a loud thump!

CHAPTER VI

THE CAT'S CUSTARD

HEARING the crash, Dinah hurried up the basement stairs. At the top she met Mrs. Bobbsey.

"What happened?" the cook asked, trying to catch her breath.

"I don't know," Mrs. Bobbsey replied. "I just came in the back door. It sounded as if one of the children had fallen downstairs!"

Together the two women ran into the front hall. There at the foot of the stairs lay Flossie. Her face was white and her eyes closed.

"Flossie! Flossie!" Mrs. Bobbsey cried fearfully.

The little girl opened her eyes and sat up unsteadily. "My head hurts," she replied. "I—I feel kind of sick."

By this time the other children and Mr. Bobbsey had arrived. The twins' father examined the chubby little girl. No bones had been broken by the fall. Mr. Bobbsey gently picked up Flossie and carried her to a sofa in the living room.

"Lie still awhile, dear," he advised.

Flossie tried hard to keep back her tears as she said, "That mean old mop handle tripped me!"

"What were you doing with a mop handle?" Mrs. Bobbsey asked in bewilderment.

Nan spoke up. "It's part of a Christmas secret, Mother."

Mrs. Bobbsey looked at her husband, then said, "In that case, I'd better not ask any more questions. The rest of you go on with whatever you were doing. I'll stay here with Flossie."

By the next morning the little girl was feeling well once more. She joined her sister and brothers on their snowy walk to school. All the way they discussed their Christmas gift project.

"If we're going to do part of it at school," Bert said, "we'll have to ask our teacher's permission."

"That's right," Nan agreed. "Let's tell Miss Moore what we're planning. I'm sure she'll help us." All the pupils in Nan and Bert's classroom liked the friendly, pleasant young woman.

It was agreed that the four Bobbseys would meet after school and talk to Miss Moore. In the meantime the conversation among all the pupils during free periods was about the coming snow-sculpture contest. Most of the children were planning to enter it.

"Wait until you see mine!" Danny Rugg bragged. "First-prize Danny—that's me every time!"

"You'll have to prove that," Charlie Mason retorted.

When school was dismissed for the day, Freddie and Flossie joined the older twins in Miss Moore's room. The pretty teacher greeted them warmly.

"How nice to see all the Bobbsey twins together!" she exclaimed. "You look as though you had something very important and very exciting on your minds."

"We do," Nan admitted, "but we need your help to carry it out."

"I'll be glad to do whatever I can. Tell me about it."

With frequent interruptions from Freddie and Flossie, Bert and Nan described their plan for *Project Santa Claus*.

"Why, I think that's wonderful, children!" Miss Moore exclaimed. "It's a lovely idea and you may certainly use the large room down the hall and also the contents of the cupboards."

The twins thanked her and said they would like to use the room the next day after school. Later, as they came out of the building to start home, Nan made a suggestion.

"Let's walk around and see what some of the others are going to do for the contest," she said. "Nellie told me she had a good idea for her entry."

The twins started off for Nellie's, stopping occasionally to toss a snowball at one another. When the Bobbseys reached Nellie's home a little later, they found their classmate rolling a snowball in her front yard.

"Want to help?" she cried, waving a greeting to the twins. "I have a terrific plan for my snow scene. It's to do with the fairy-tale figures of Cinderella and Prince Charming."

"Oh dear!" Nan groaned in dismay.

Nellie looked at her friend, puzzled. "What's the matter? Don't you think a fairy-tale scene is a good idea?"

Quickly Nan explained that the Bobbseys had thought of doing the same thing. "But we'll make something else," she added.

The twins waved good-by and continued their walk. "What can we make now, Bert?" Freddie asked anxiously.

"Why don't we combine your idea and mine and model Santa and a reindeer?" Bert suggested.

"That would be great!" Freddie agreed enthusiastically.

They walked on down the street and presently came in sight of Charlie Mason's house. "There he is!" Flossie cried. "He's making a big snowball."

"Hi, Charlie!" Bert hailed his friend. "Is this the beginning of your snow sculpture?"

Three large snowballs stood side by side on the lawn and he was rolling a fourth.

"Yes." Charlie paused and brushed the snow from his mittens. "I've decided to make Santa Claus in a sleigh."

The four Bobbsey children began to laugh.

"What's so funny?" Charlie asked suspiciously. "That's a good Christmas subject."

"It sure is!" Bert agreed when he had stopped laughing. "We were going to do it ourselves!"

Charlie grinned when Nan and Bert told him about Nellie's having picked their first choice for her sculpture. "Now you've taken our second!"

"Don't worry," he said. "If I know you Bobbseys, you'll come up with something which will beat us all!"

"Well, we'll have to use the old brains to do it," Bert remarked as they resumed their walk. "It won't be easy."

On the way the twins passed several other snow scenes which had been started. They were told the sculptures would be snowmen, sleighs, reindeers, and Santas.

Flossie was near tears. "What are we going to do?" she wailed.

"Don't worry, Flossie," Nan consoled her little sister. "We'll talk about it this evening with Mother and Dad. One of us is sure to think of something."

When the children reached home they went at once to the third-floor playroom to resume work on their secret project.

Once more Bert consulted his list. "This last thing we need—Freddie, you were going to get it. Remember?"

"That's right. I think I saw some in the basement," Freddie replied. "I'll get them now."

But when Freddie reached the kitchen and opened the door to the basement stairs he heard his mother's voice. She was talking to Dinah in the laundry.

"I'll have to wait until they come up," he decided.

At that moment their black cat, Snoop, came

bounding up the steps, his tail waving. He stopped in front of the little boy and began to *meow.*

"Maybe Snoop's hungry," Freddie thought. "I'll get him some milk."

He opened the refrigerator door and reached for a bottle. But in doing this he hit a bowl of custard which Dinah had baked for supper. Freddie made a wild grab for the bowl but was too late! It slipped from his hand and fell to the floor with a crash! The creamy contents flew in all directions.

At the sound Snoop quickly retreated under the table, but in a moment he cautiously advanced and soon was happily lapping up the custard.

"Freddie! What are you doing?" The question came from Mrs. Bobbsey, who had run up the steps when she heard the noise in the kitchen. Dinah was close behind her.

"I—I'm sorry, Mother," Freddie cried. "I was just going to give Snoop some milk and all this custard fell out of the refrigerator!"

"Well, you'd better help Dinah clean up the mess and then run upstairs and play with the other children before you do any more damage here," Mrs. Bobbsey advised.

So, without doing his errand, Freddie trudged up the stairs. When he reported his mishap to his brother and sisters, Flossie giggled.

"Snoop had an extra meal even if you didn't get the things in the basement!"

After Freddie had gone upstairs, Dinah turned toward Mrs. Bobbsey, a puzzled expression on her face. "Why didn't you tell Freddie about what we found downstairs? I had all I could do to keep from blurting it out!"

"Well, Dinah, I'm not sure, but I have a hunch they may be the surprise that the children are saving for Richard and me, and I don't want to spoil their fun. I think I'll hint around at dinner tonight," Mrs. Bobbsey said.

During the evening meal the talk again turned to Christmas plans. Suddenly, with a smile on her face Mrs. Bobbsey asked, "Is the secret you children are planning somewhere in the basement?"

Bert, Nan, Freddie, and Flossie looked at one another in bewilderment.

CHAPTER VII

THE SNOW CASTLE

THEIR secret in the basement? What could Mrs. Bobbsey have in mind?

"Why, no, Mother," Nan replied. "What makes you think so?"

"Flossie and Freddie seem to be around there more than usual," Mrs. Bobbsey said. Then with a twinkle in her eyes she added, "Maybe it's just Dinah's and my secret!"

Though the children teased her, she refused to say any more and the conversation turned to the snow-sculpture contest.

"Everyone's doing fairy-tale scenes!" Nan wailed.

"I'm sure we can figure out something else," Mr. Bobbsey remarked. "Your mother and I are going out this evening. But you children put your thinking caps on and we'll discuss what to do tomorrow night."

With their parents away, the twins decided it was a good time to work on their special project, and bedtime came far too soon.

"Remember we'll meet in the big room tomorrow after school," Nan cautioned the younger twins.

As Bert and Nan walked home from classes the next noon, another thought occurred to Nan. She stopped short. "Bert," she said, "we'll need a fifth person! Don't you remember?"

The boy snapped his fingers. "That's right! But who would do it?"

"How about Nellie Parks?"

"Great!" Bert approved. "And why don't we let Charlie in on it too? I think we need someone to keep an eye on Danny so he won't be spying on us."

"That's a good idea," Nan agreed. "Let's ask them as soon as we get back to school!"

Before the afternoon classes began Bert and Nan managed to get Charlie and Nellie away from the other children. The twins outlined *Project Santa Claus* and asked their friends to help.

Nellie was delighted with her suggested part in the plan. Charlie, too, was enthusiastic.

"I'll bring my books and do my homework in the room just across the hall from where you'll be. That way I can keep watch and let you know if Danny comes around," he proposed.

When classes were over for the day and most of the children had left, the twins and Nellie went into the big room and soon were deep in work on the project.

Charlie settled down in the room across the hall. He chose a desk by the window from which he had a clear view of the room opposite, but where he probably would not be noticed by anyone passing in the hall. In a few moments he was busy with an arithmetic problem.

Then suddenly he heard a noise in the hall. Charlie looked up from his book. There was Danny Rugg, his ear pressed to the door of the big room.

"Of all the nerve!" Charlie muttered to himself as he quietly got up from his chair and started for the hall.

But before Charlie could reach the door, Danny had straightened up and tiptoed away. Charlie went back to the desk where he was studying, and picked up his book.

Five minutes later, however, Danny returned, this time carrying a straight wooden chair. Peering about furtively, he quietly set the chair in front of the door and stepped up onto the seat.

Charlie chuckled to himself. "Danny's going

to try to peek through the transom," he thought, "but he'll never make it."

The bully soon realized this too. He climbed down from the chair and left. In a few minutes he came back, this time lugging a large dictionary and two other thick books. These he placed on the chair.

Carefully Danny climbed up onto the books. Then, steadying himself against the wall, he raised up on his toes to peer through the glass at the top of the door.

Charlie had walked quietly to the hall. Before Danny had a chance to peek, Charlie said sternly, "What do you think you're doing, Danny Rugg?"

Crash! Bang! Thump!

Danny, books, and chair tumbled to the floor! The door flew open and the Bobbseys and Nellie ran out. They gazed in amazement at the red-faced boy. Across the hall, Charlie was doubled up with laughter.

"Ha! Ha!" he cried when he could speak again. "What were you looking at, Danny?"

The bully picked himself up and glowered at Charlie. "You're not supposed to be in these rooms after school," he muttered. "I was trying to see what those sneaky Bobbseys were doing."

"We have permission to be in these rooms,

Danny, books, and chair
tumbled to the floor!

Danny Rugg!" Nan said indignantly. "And anyway it's none of your business what we're doing!"

"Is that so?" Danny asked sneeringly. "Don't forget I *know* what you're doing and I think it's crazy!"

After Danny had left, scowling and promising to get even with Charlie, Bert said, "I guess we'd better call it a day now." He grinned. "We'd never be able to work without thinking of Danny on the floor!"

The others laughed and agreed.

"See you tomorrow!" Nellie called later as she turned down her street. "I love being in on the project!"

That evening in the Bobbsey living room the family talked about what they could do to enter the snow-sculpture contest. Mr. and Mrs. Bobbsey suggested numerous subjects, but each time one of the twins would cry, "It's already being done!"

"Why don't we make a snow castle?" Flossie said finally.

"That's just the thing!" Nan cried. "We can find a picture of a simple one and copy it."

After a few minutes' discussion, all the Bobbseys agreed that a snow castle would be the best entry they could think of for the contest.

"Look on the bookshelves, Nan," Mrs. Bobbsey urged. "I think we have a book on castles."

"Here it is!" Nan brought back a large volume. She and Bert bent over it, turning the pages until Nan exclaimed, "Here's one!"

The picture she showed her mother and father was of a medieval stone castle built around a large courtyard. At each corner of the building stood a square tower.

"That's neat!" Bert agreed. "It could be made very easily out of snow."

Mr. Bobbsey got a pad and pencil and began to sketch a simple form for the castle. The twins gathered around him and watched as the pencil flew over the paper.

"That's great, Dad!" Freddie said admiringly. The twins' father thought the snow castle should have walls of giant snowballs. The front and back walls would be ten feet long, and the sides six feet deep.

"A square tower at each corner and a doorway in the center," he said.

"How high will the walls be?" Bert asked.

"Oh, five and a half feet," his father answered. "I think that size will fit very nicely on our front lawn."

Suddenly Bert had an idea. With a meaningful wink at Nan he proposed, "Why not build our castle on the school lawn?"

Mr. Bobbsey looked surprised. "Why do that,

Bert? The entries are supposed to be built at the homes of Lakeport residents."

Nan also had looked puzzled, but now her face broke into a smile. She thought she knew why Bert had made this suggestion. The snow castle could be used in *Project Santa Claus!*

The small twins looked from Bert to Nan, then suddenly Flossie clapped her hands. "I think that's a scrumptious idea," she exclaimed.

"So do I," Freddie agreed.

Bert went on. "We can enter our sculpture in the name of Lakeport School and then if we should win the prize, the money would go to the school!"

"Yes," Nan agreed. "We're always trying to raise money for the Library Fund. This might be a good way to do it."

Mrs. Bobbsey turned to her husband and smiled. "You know, Dick," she said, "I think we should be very proud of our children."

Mr. Bobbsey nodded. "I agree, Mary. Okay, Bert. It's a fine idea. We'll build the snow castle on the school lawn if you can get Mr. Tetlow's approval."

Bert offered to go to the principal's office the next day and ask his permission.

"If he agrees," said Mr. Bobbsey, "we'll start work next week. We don't want to build the castle too far ahead of the judging. There might possibly be a thaw."

"When it's finished, I'm going to guard it," Freddie announced stoutly. "Nobody's going to storm our castle!"

At this moment Dinah appeared at the door and beckoned to Mrs. Bobbsey.

"What is it, Dinah?" the twins' mother asked, somewhat perplexed.

But Dinah did not answer. Instead she shook her head mysteriously and, beckoning once more, disappeared.

Mrs. Bobbsey arose from her chair with a little laugh. "Well, I guess I'll have to see what this is all about."

She left the room, and Mr. Bobbsey, although curious, settled back and began to read the evening paper. The twins were mystified too, but soon began to discuss the school Christmas program. The holidays were to start on Wednesday of the following week. There would be no classes, but a simple program of Christmas music, including songs by the children, had been planned for the morning Assembly.

"What are the little children going to do?" Nan asked Freddie and Flossie. "I hear that the Junior Choir is singing."

"Yes," Freddie replied with an important air.

"We're all going to sing a couple of songs. And Flossie and I stand in the front row of the choir."

"And Teddy Blake and Susie Larker are going to sing a funny song!" Flossie added, her eyes sparkling. "Miss Burns said they might!"

"Boy, everybody will burst out laughing when they hear it!" Freddie added.

Nan asked what the name of the funny song was, but before the small twins could reply, Mrs. Bobbsey came back into the living room. With a smile on her face, she announced to the children, "I have something special to show you! Come with me."

CHAPTER VIII

FIRE!

AT MRS. BOBBSEY'S announcement that she had something to show the twins, they hastily followed her.

"What is it, Mother?" Flossie whispered in excitement.

Mrs. Bobbsey put three fingers to her lips and shook her head. "Wait and you'll see!" she said.

She led the children out through the kitchen and down the basement stairs. When they reached the furnace room she paused.

"Look there!" she exclaimed and pointed to a far corner.

Freddie and Flossie ran to the spot. "Oh! Baby kittens!" Flossie cried.

On a piece of old, frayed carpet lay a large white mother cat surrounded by five little black-and-white kittens! Snoop stood beside them, his tail proudly switching.

"Snoop's their daddy?" Freddie asked. When his mother nodded, he grabbed up their pet and hugged him.

The other children were bending over, stroking the tiny babies and their mother.

"They're darling!" Nan cried.

"Didn't you really know about them, children?" Mrs. Bobbsey asked.

"No, Mother. Honestly," Nan assured her. Then she added, "Is this what you meant when you asked us if our Christmas secret was in the basement?"

"Yes. Dinah discovered the kittens and showed them to me yesterday. When you children seemed to have so much business down here, I thought perhaps you had found them and were saving the kittens for a Christmas surprise for your father and me," Mrs. Bobbsey explained.

"How did the mother kitty get in here?" Freddie asked. "Snoop couldn't open the door."

Dinah had followed the family down the steps. Now she laughed. "I let her in," she admitted. "And yesterday her babies were born." The cook sighed. "I suppose we'll have to put them out."

"Oh no!" the twins chorused in horror, and

Flossie added, "Snoop would be hurt if we didn't take care of his family!"

"Yes," said Nan. "And we'll have to make sure that Snap doesn't come down here and bother them."

"Oh, look!" Bert said, laughing, as one particularly adventurous kitten wriggled off the carpet and tried to stand up.

When the mother cat and her kittens went to sleep, the twins climbed up to the first floor.

"Tomorrow's a school day," Mrs. Bobbsey reminded them a little later. "I think it's time you children said good night."

They sleepily agreed and it was not long before they were in bed. The next morning when the Bobbseys awoke they found there had been another snowfall. The fresh layer glistened on the branches of trees and shrubs.

"More work for you, Bert!" Nan teased as they walked to school. "You'll have to shovel this afternoon."

"I'm glad," her brother replied. "Every new snow means more money for *Project Santa Claus!*"

"Maybe some of it you won't collect," Freddie remarked. "I saw the Walker family drive away early this morning in their new station wagon. Mother says they won't be back 'til New Year's!"

The Walkers lived a few doors down the street from the Bobbseys and were one of the families that had engaged Bert to keep their walks clear.

Bert looked disappointed. "Good night!" he exclaimed. "That means I won't get paid until after Christmas! Still, I promised to clear the walks so I'll have to do it."

When they reached school, Charlie Mason ran up to Bert. He was grinning broadly.

"Danny sure is mad about yesterday afternoon," Charlie reported with relish. "He told Jack Westley that he was going to get even with you and me if it was the last thing he did!"

"Danny's always trying to get even," Bert scoffed. "I'm not afraid of him!"

"Just the same, keep your eyes open," Charlie advised. "You know Danny can play some pretty mean tricks!"

Bert promised to be careful. However, during the day Danny seemed to be keeping away from the Bobbseys. He merely scowled when Nan met him in the hall and hurried on without a word.

After school Nan, Freddie, and Flossie went directly to Aunt Sally Pry's to help her with the Christmas candies. Freddie followed his sisters into the house.

"Hello, Aunt Sally," he called. "Have you anything to deliver?"

The sweet old lady came into the hall, busily tying on a fresh apron.

"What makes me quiver?" she replied. "I'm not quivering. Why do you ask?"

Freddie laughed and ran up to her. Putting his mouth close to her ear, he repeated his question.

Aunt Sally hugged the little boy. "Bless your heart," she said. "I have lots of boxes for you to deliver."

"I'll go home and get my sled," Freddie said joyfully and ran out of the house.

When he reached home he found Snap playing in the back yard. Watching the dog leaping happily through the snowdrifts, Freddie had an idea.

He ran into the garage where not only his sled was kept, but also an old harness. The children had bought this for Snap the year before.

"Here, Snap!" he called. The dog bounded up, and in a few minutes Freddie had harnessed his pet to the sled. Then he hopped on and proudly drove off to Aunt Sally's.

Flossie was near the kitchen window when Freddie came around the corner of Mrs. Pry's house.

"Oh, look!" she cried as her twin stopped with a flourish. "Freddie has a dog-horse!"

Nan and Aunt Sally hurried to the window. They laughed as they watched Freddie get off the sled and solemnly tie Snap's harness to a corner of the porch.

Nan had already tied the candy boxes into several bundles. The two girls fastened them onto the sled. As Snap trotted off, Freddie ran alongside the load.

"This is the Bobbsey Express!" he called as he waved good-by.

In the meantime Bert had hurried home from school to get his snow shovel. "I'll do the two houses between us and the Walkers first," he decided. "After all, the Walkers aren't home so it won't matter if I can't finish their walks this afternoon."

For two hours he worked industriously. It was growing dark by the time he reached the Walkers' small colonial house. He had cleared the soft new snow from the front walk and part of the drive when he glanced toward the back door.

The upper part of the door was made of glass. Through the glass Bert could see a flickering light.

Startled, he muttered to himself, "What

could that be? I wonder if the Walkers forgot and left a light on!"

He ran up the back steps and peered into the kitchen. An ironing board had been set up near the back door. At the end where the iron was placed a tiny flame had started. Apparently Mrs. Walker had been ironing before they left and had forgotten to pull out the plug!

Bert caught his breath. What should he do? If he ran home to call the fire department, the little flame might spread and cause a big fire.

"I'll just have to break in!" he told himself desperately.

Shielding his face with his muffler, Bert smashed the glass with the handle of the snow shovel. Then, reaching in through the jagged hole, he slipped the lock and opened the door.

Bert quickly tore the electric cord from the wall socket and with one heave tossed both board and iron out into the snow!

"Wow!" he gasped.

Still shaking from excitement, Bert made his way home. When he reached the house Mr. Bobbsey was just driving into the garage.

"Hi, son!" he called, climbing out of the car and coming toward Bert. "You look upset. What's the matter?"

Bert told his story. "Good for you!" his

father praised him. "I'd say that was quick thinking! I'll walk back with you now to make sure everything else is all right and then we'll have Sam board up that door until the Walkers get home."

Together they examined the Walker kitchen. There was no damage and no sign of fire.

"I guess you got here just in time!" Mr. Bobbsey said, slapping his son on the back.

At the supper table Bert described his experience. Freddie and Flossie listened wide-eyed.

"Oh, Bert, you're a real hero!" Flossie cried.

Freddie nodded in agreement. "If I'd only been there with my fire engine, we could have put out the fire right in the house!" he exclaimed regretfully.

"We're all very proud of you, Bert," Mrs. Bobbsey said, "and I know the Walkers will be very grateful."

Later in the evening Flossie found an opportunity to whisper to Freddie. "Remember the things in the basement? You never got them!"

"That's right! I'll get them now," he promised.

When Freddie went into the kitchen, Dinah and Sam were there. Without saying anything to them, Freddie opened the door to the basement.

"Where you going, Freddie?" the cook asked.

The little boy hesitated, then answered, "I'm going to say good night to Snoop's children."

"Well, don't stay down there too long," Dinah advised. "Those kittens need their sleep."

Freddie tiptoed down the stairs and around into the furnace room. The mother cat and her kittens were fast asleep! Freddie stooped down and stroked them gently.

"Now I'll get what I came for," he told himself. He walked into the laundry room and glanced around. The things he was looking for were not there!

He ran up the stairs and back into the living

room. Flossie was working a puzzle in one corner. Freddie walked over and began to help her.

"They're gone!" he whispered.

"We need them!" Flossie insisted. "I guess you'll just have to ask Mother!"

"Okay." Freddie looked resigned. He walked over to the sofa where Mrs. Bobbsey sat reading.

"Mother," he said hesitantly, "may I have two sheets?"

CHAPTER IX

LOCKED IN!

"SHEETS!" Mrs. Bobbsey repeated in surprise as she looked up from the book she was reading. "Why do you want sheets, Freddie?"

Her small son looked at the floor and shifted from one foot to the other. "Won't you just give them to me?" he said evasively. "I won't hurt them and I'll explain later."

Mrs. Bobbsey laughed. "More Christmas secrets?" she asked. "All right, you may take two old ones out of the linen closet, but please be careful not to tear them."

"Oh, thank you, Mother!" both Freddie and Flossie cried and ran out of the room.

Bert and Nan grinned at each other and stood up. "I guess we'll go upstairs, too, Mother," Nan said. "Good night."

After the twins had gone Mrs. Bobbsey looked at her husband and smiled. "The children are planning some kind of surprise for us at Christmas, I think. Freddie must be going to play ghost!"

"Ghosts and Christmas don't seem to go together," Mr. Bobbsey protested, laughing, "but you never can tell what our children are going to do!"

The Christmas surprise was still uppermost in the twins' minds as they walked back to school after lunch the next day. "Mr. Tetlow has called a rehearsal for the Senior Choir after classes this afternoon," Nan told the younger twins, "so we won't be able to work very long on our project. But come to the big room for a little while and we'll do as much as we can."

The twins and Nellie worked hard on the surprise after classes were out. They were making great headway when Charlie knocked on the door of the big room.

"Hey, you kids," he called, "they're calling our chorus rehearsal now. Come on!"

"Okay," Bert replied.

"We'll have to stop," Nan told the small twins. "You'd better go on home, and tell Mother why we're late."

After the older children had gone off to the rehearsal, Freddie and Flossie amused themselves a little longer with the project. Then

Freddie grew restless. He wandered into the room used by the kindergarten children, which connected with the one in which they were working.

In a minute he called to Flossie. "Come in here and see something!"

Flossie ran to where her brother was standing. On the floor stood a little white fence surrounding an area about three feet square. It was covered with artificial grass. Ten tiny, yellow chicks were chirping and busily picking up bits of seed from the grass.

"Oh, how darling!" Flossie exclaimed, crouching down to get a better look. "I'd love to have one!"

Freddie reached over the little fence and picked up one of the fluffy balls. "Here you are," he said.

"Oh, Freddie, we can't take one!" Flossie protested. "But isn't he sweet?" She brushed the soft little chick against her cheek before putting it back with the others.

"And look here!" Freddie called from the other side of the room. He pointed to a large glass aquarium. Small plants swayed in the bottom of the tank and fish of many kinds swam lazily in the greenish water.

"They're bee-yoo-ti-ful!" Flossie exclaimed as

she peered at the fish. There were some which looked paper thin, surrounded by delicate fins which waved as they swam. Others had large, protruding eyes and Flossie giggled as they came toward her. Freddie saw an angel fish and also four or five tiny black ones which darted to and fro through the water.

While Flossie admired the tropical fish, Freddie wandered around the room. On a shelf he noticed what looked like a shoe box with holes punched in it.

"I wonder what this is!" he called to his twin.

The shelf was high and as he reached to take the box in his hand, it slipped from his fingers. It fell to the floor and the lid came off.

Two tiny gray mice leaped out!

"Eek!" Flossie exclaimed as her twin tried to grab the little creatures. But they scurried away, far out of reach!

"Flossie! Help me!" Freddie wailed. "I have to put them back in their box."

They were the fastest moving mice the children had ever seen. They scurried around the edge of the floor, their little whiskers and pink noses twitching furiously.

Freddie and Flossie got down on their hands and knees to chase the little animals. Just as Freddie thought he had one cornered and put out his hand to pick it up, the little mouse gave a leap. It landed on a drapery which hung at the side of the window!

Flossie was busy trying to capture the second mouse. This one also ran up the drapery.

"Bring the box, Flossie!" Freddie cried. "Maybe we can shake the curtain and make the mice fall in!"

Flossie held the box against the drapery while

Freddie shook it gently. In a second there were two little *plops* and the mice landed in the box. Quickly Flossie slammed on the lid!

During all this time the school janitor had been making his rounds. He looked into the big room and, since he saw no one there, closed and locked the door.

"I guess all the children have gone home," he told himself, and shuffled off to his basement workroom.

A few minutes later Freddie and Flossie came back into the big room. "We'd better go home," Flossie remarked. "Nan wanted us to tell Mother why she and Bert would be late."

"Okay," Freddie agreed.

The twins pulled on their heavy coats and hats with ear muffs. Then they walked over to open the door. It would not move. Freddie shook the door but it still would not open.

"We're locked in, Flossie!" the little boy cried.

"Locked in!" Flossie repeated. "How could we be? The door was open a little while ago!"

"Well, it's locked now," Freddie said. "Try it yourself!"

Flossie did so, but the door did not budge. "How are we going to get out?" she asked worriedly.

"Don't worry," Freddie said. "I'll find a way."

He looked around the room and his eyes fell on the door to the kindergarten room. "Come on," he called. "We can go out that way."

Together the children ran back into the room where they had seen the chickens and fish and mice. Flossie tried the door which led into the hall. It, too, was locked.

"We can't get out this way either," she said, her lower lip beginning to quiver.

"What about the windows?" Freddie suggested. "I can climb out and find somebody to unlock the door."

The twins walked around the room, studying the windows. They were all locked and the catches were too far up for the children to reach.

"No good," Freddie sighed.

"What shall we do now?" Flossie asked.

"Let's yell," Freddie suggested. "Maybe if we scream, someone will hear us."

So they called and called at the top of their voices, but no one came. They did not realize it, but the rehearsal had broken up and all the members of the choir had left the school.

"Oh dear," Flossie sighed. "It's beginning to get dark and I think everybody must have gone home. We'll have to stay here all night!" She looked despairingly around the room.

Then suddenly her eyes lighted on a wall telephone. "Freddie!" she cried. "The phone! We can use it to call someone!"

"Good!" Freddie exclaimed. He ran over and picked up the instrument. Then he groaned in disappointment. "Oh, Flossie, this is just an inside phone. The only place we can call is Mr. Tetlow's office!"

"Well, try it anyway. Maybe Mr. Tetlow is still here."

Freddie pushed the button which buzzed the principal's office. There was no response. Flossie tried her luck and rang it several times, but still there was no answer.

Tears rolled down Flossie's cheeks. "Nan and Bert thought we left school right after they did! Oh, Freddie! No one will know where we are! What'll we ever do?"

"Don't be upset, Flossie," her brother urged, determined to be brave. "Mr. Carter, the janitor, stays real late. We'll just keep on trying the phone. Maybe he'll hear it ringing." Freddie pushed the buzzer again and again.

In the meantime Bert and Nan had arrived home. After telling Mrs. Bobbsey about the rehearsal and describing the songs they were to sing, Nan asked her mother, "Where are Freddie and Flossie?"

Mrs. Bobbsey looked startled. "Why, I thought they stayed at school to wait for you! You mean they didn't come home with you and Bert?"

Oh, no," Bert spoke up. "I'm sure Flossie and Freddie left when we went to rehearsal."

"They probably stopped at Susie's or Teddy's to play," Nan said reassuringly. "I think I'll go upstairs and start my homework."

"And I'd better do some more snow shoveling," Bert declared, and went outside.

A short time later Mrs. Bobbsey called up to Nan, "I'm going to phone Susie and Teddy and see if the twins are at either place. It's beginning to get dark and they certainly should be home by this time."

Really worried now, Nan ran down the stairs and waited while her mother called the Larkers' and the Blakes' homes. She was told that the twins had not been there. Mrs. Bobbsey quickly got in touch with other friends of Freddie and Flossie, but none of them knew where the small twins were.

Nan and her mother looked at each other in dismay, wondering what to do next. Just then Bert came in. "Oh, Bert!" Nan cried. "Freddie and Flossie haven't come home yet! We can't imagine where they are. They're not at any of their friends' houses!"

"I only hope they haven't fallen into deep snow," Mrs. Bobbsey said uneasily, thinking of the many large drifts at curbs and in uncleared areas.

"Well, what are we waiting for, Nan?" Bert said. "Let's go look for them!"

CHAPTER X

A MISCHIEVOUS PET

AS NAN went for her coat, the front doorbell rang, then again and again. The caller was impatient!

"Oh dear, I hope no one's bringing us bad news!" Mrs. Bobbsey cried.

Quickly Bert opened the door. There stood Mr. Carter, the school janitor. And on each side of him stood one of the small twins!

"Freddie! Flossie! I'm so glad you're home!" their mother exclaimed. "Are you all right?"

As the twins nodded, Mr. Carter said, "They're all right, ma'am, but I just about fixed it so they'd have to stay in school all night!"

"We got locked in!" Freddie said and explained what had happened. "But we kept on ringing Mr. Tetlow's office on the telephone," he concluded, "and finally Mr. Carter answered!"

"That's right," the janitor agreed. "I was working in the basement and couldn't hear the phone until I went upstairs to make my final rounds before going home."

"We were glad when he came to let us out," Flossie cried.

Mrs. Bobbsey smiled. "It was very good of you to bring the twins home, Mr. Carter," she said. "Thank you so much."

"That's all right, ma'am," the janitor replied. "They're nice children and I wanted to be sure they got home safe." With a final pat on the head for Freddie and Flossie, Mr. Carter left.

Now that their adventure had ended happily, the small twins began to enjoy the attention they were getting. They entertained their father at supper by telling him all about the incident. He laughed heartily at the mice-catching operation.

"I'm glad everything turned out all right," Mr. Bobbsey remarked, "but I don't think you should stay at school after classes unless you have some special reason."

"But we—" Flossie began, then stopped, her hand to her mouth.

"We had a rehearsal for the Christmas program," Nan put in, hoping that her little sister's slip would go unnoticed.

This turned the conversation to the school entertainment and no more was said about Freddie and Flossie's adventure.

The next day after classes Nan and Flossie stopped at home before going on to Aunt Sally Pry's. As they were preparing to leave the house, Snoop walked into the room. When he saw the girls he gave a plaintive *meow*.

Flossie bent down and scooped up the pet in her arms. "Let's take him with us, Nan!" she said. "Snoop hasn't seen Aunt Sally in a long time."

"All right," Nan agreed.

Flossie put her pet down and opened the front door. "Do you want to come with us, Snoop?" she asked.

For answer the black cat ran down the front walk, then paused to look back at the girls as if to say, "Come on, let's go!"

Nan and Flossie caught up with him, and Snoop bounded along proudly beside them. When they reached Mrs. Pry's house, she opened the door.

"Come in," she said. "I'm glad to see you."

"May Snoop come in, too?" Flossie asked. "We brought him for a treat."

"He wants some meat?" Aunt Sally said. "I don't think I have any meat for him, but there's plenty of milk."

Flossie giggled. "I didn't say he wanted meat. I said he was having a treat!"

"Oh!" Aunt Sally laughed. "That's fine. I'm glad to see him!"

The two girls followed the elderly woman into her kitchen. She took two gay, printed aprons from a drawer.

"Put these on," she directed. "We can't have you getting your pretty dresses sticky!"

"What would you like me to do first?" Nan asked.

"Here is the recipe for fudge," Aunt Sally replied. "You might just measure out all the ingredients and then we'll be ready to start the mixing."

Mrs. Pry brought in several trays of finished candies from the pantry and put them down beside Flossie. "These are all ready to pack, dear," she said.

Carefully Flossie tore off waxed paper and lined each box. Then she gently put each piece of candy into a little fluted paper cup and placed it in the box. As each was filled she put on the lids and tied them with Christmas ribbon. On the top she placed a bow.

"Don't they look pretty?" she asked, stepping back to admire her work.

"Yes, they certainly do, Flossie," Aunt Sally agreed. "You're a very good packer."

She turned to Nan. "How are you getting on with that Christmas project you told me about?"

"Just fine, Aunt Sally," Nan replied. "We've been working on it every day and next week it will be finished."

"Did you find everything you needed?" the woman asked.

Nan hesitated, then admitted that there was one problem they had not yet been able to solve. When she explained what it was, Mrs. Pry looked thoughtful for a moment. Then she said, "I may be able to help you. When we finish this batch of candy, we'll go upstairs and see what I have."

"Thank you, Aunt Sally," Nan cried. "That will be great!"

Flossie came over to watch the bubbling mass of chocolate in the big kettle. "When will it be done?" she asked, sniffing the delicious aroma.

"When the line in the thermometer gets to that point," Nan explained, pointing to a figure on the candy thermometer fastened to the edge of the pan.

Flossie watched breathlessly. Then she exclaimed, "There it is! The line is at that spot!"

Nan carefully removed the kettle from the flame while Aunt Sally brought a long, shallow pan, the bottom of which was covered with nut meats. Nan ladled out the rich chocolate mixture over them.

"Oh, that looks scrumptious!" Flossie cried.

"We'll let it cool before we cut the fudge," Mrs. Pry said. "In the meantime, let's go upstairs and see what we can find for your project."

She led the way into a storage room and lifted the lid of an old-fashioned trunk which stood in one corner.

"I used to have a boarder who had been an actress," Aunt Sally explained. "When she left here she gave me this trunk and the things in it. She said she didn't want them any more."

From one end of the trunk the old lady took a long box. When she opened it, Nan and Flossie could see that it was filled with bracelets, necklaces, and strings of various colored beads.

"Don't you wear them?" Flossie asked.

"Oh, you can't tear them," Aunt Sally replied. "Whatever made you think of that?"

Nan smiled and leaned closer to Mrs. Pry. "Flossie asked if you ever wear them," she explained in a louder voice.

"There I go again!" Aunt Sally laughed.

"No, I don't wear them. How would an old lady like me look in all that flashy jewelry?"

"I think you'd look lovely," Flossie declared, throwing her arms around Aunt Sally.

Mrs. Pry patted the little girl affectionately, then turned to Nan. "Do you think you could use the beads?" she asked.

"Oh, yes!" Nan exclaimed. "They'd be perfect!"

"Well, take them along. You're welcome to them."

"Thank you, Aunt Sally! Bert and Freddie will be thrilled, too!" Nan said.

The three went downstairs and Flossie ran to the kitchen. At the door she stopped short.

"Wh—what happened?" she cried.

Aunt Sally and Nan came up behind her. They too cried out in astonishment.

The white boxes of candy were scattered helter-skelter on the table and each beautiful red bow had been untied! The ribbon from one box was missing entirely.

"Who could have been in here?" Aunt Sally asked in bewilderment. "And why would anyone do such a thing? It doesn't make sense!"

Suddenly Nan began to laugh. "Where is Snoop?" she asked.

"Oh, Nan, do you think he did it?" Flossie cried.

"I wouldn't be surprised. You know how he likes to get a piece of ribbon to play with."

Seeing that Aunt Sally still looked puzzled, Nan explained their suspicions. "Well, let's hunt for him," the old lady proposed. "He may be making more trouble."

They looked under tables and chairs and behind the sofa in the living room but Snoop was not found. They were about to give up and return to the kitchen when Nan raised her hand, motioning Aunt Sally and Flossie to be quiet.

"I hear a queer noise in the hall. Perhaps he's there," she suggested.

Aunt Sally opened the door as quietly as possible and they tiptoed out into the entrance hall. Still there was no sign of Snoop.

Flossie, following the strange thumping sound, went to the end of the hall and peered into the space under the stairs. Then she giggled.

"Here he is!" she announced.

CHAPTER XI

AN UNFAIR RACE

"YOU'VE found Snoop?" Nan cried, as she and Aunt Sally hurried to the spot.

"Yes, and he's all mixed up," Flossie answered.

What a funny sight met their eyes. Snoop lay on his back under the stairway, his four paws in the air. He was hopelessly snarled in a long red ribbon! The black cat looked most unhappy.

"Snoop! You're a naughty boy!" Flossie scolded as she knelt down and began to unwind the ribbon from her pet.

When the cat was free, he jumped to his feet, shook his head in a quick sneeze, and raced back to the kitchen. The others followed to save the rest of the candy boxes.

But Snoop had had enough of ribbons for the moment. He sat under the table unconcernedly licking his paws and washing his face.

Nan helped Flossie retie the bows on the candy boxes and they piled them up for Freddie's next delivery.

"Good-by, Aunt Sally," Nan called as she went into the hall to get her coat. "Freddie will be here tomorrow."

"Borrow?" Aunt Sally called. "Of course, my dear, you may borrow anything I have. What do you want?"

"We don't want to borrow anything," Nan explained, coming back into the kitchen as she pulled on her wool mittens. "I said Freddie would come tomorrow to deliver the rest of the candy."

"That will be fine," Mrs. Pry remarked. "My candy business has been very good and you children have been a great help—except for Snoop." She laughed. "I'm so glad you wanted to work for me."

"It's been fun, Aunt Sally," Flossie replied, giving her an affectionate hug.

"Yes, and thank you for everything," Nan added. "They'll be just perfect for our project."

On the walk home Nan and Flossie planned how they would use the necklaces. "Oh, it's going to be bee-yoo-ti-ful!" Flossie exclaimed, "when our project is all ready."

There was more snow that night, and the next morning Freddie was at Mrs. Pry's early to make his deliveries. When he returned home he found Bert still working on the walks. Nan was helping her mother with some Christmas packages which were to be mailed to places a distance from Lakeport. Flossie was talking to Dinah in the kitchen.

Freddie beckoned to his twin. "Come on out, Flossie," he called. "I've thought of something for us to do."

Flossie hurried into her snowsuit and followed Freddie to the back yard. "What is it?" she asked.

"Let's polish the runners on our sleds!"

"Why?"

"They'll go much faster on the snow if we do," Freddie explained.

"That would be good," Flossie agreed. "How do we polish them?"

Freddie explained that he had found some sandpaper in the garage. Carefully he tore a piece of the rough coated paper in two and handed one part to Flossie.

Then he turned his sled over. "See," he said, pointing to some small flecks of rust on the steel runners, "I'll rub the sandpaper hard on the runners and take off all that rust. Then I'll be able to speed down any hill."

Flossie brought her sled out and soon the two curly blond heads were bent over their work. In a few minutes Freddie had finished his cleaning job.

"I think I'll do Bert's, too," he decided, and went off to get the other sled. In a moment he was back.

By that time Flossie, too, had finished. "I'll fix Nan's sled," she told her twin. "But let's keep it as a s'prise and not tell them!"

"Okay," Freddie agreed.

The children worked hard until Dinah called them to lunch.

"What have you two been doing all morning?" Nan asked as the family sat down at the dining-room table.

Freddie and Flossie looked at each other and Flossie put her finger to her lips. "It's a secret," she said, her blue eyes dancing.

Mrs. Bobbsey laughed. "My, our house is exciting at this time of year," she said. "Everyone has secrets from everyone else. I even have a few myself!"

"Oh, Mother, tell us your secrets," Flossie begged.

But Mrs. Bobbsey shook her head. "You'll learn them at Christmas—not before."

When lunch was over the twins hurried to the hill for an afternoon of coasting with their friends, some of whom were already there.

"Let's have a race!" Charlie Mason called when he saw the Bobbseys approaching.

"Okay," Freddie agreed. "I'll bet my sled can go faster than anybody's!"

"Well, we'll see," Charlie replied.

The five children lined up at the top of the

hill, their sleds held tightly. Then at a signal from Bert, they ran forward, throwing themselves down onto the sleds. The long coast down the hill began.

Freddie was the last to start and the others sped ahead of him. "Come on, Freddie!" he urged himself, "I must win!"

Suddenly he saw a small hump ahead to the left of the run. Taking a chance, the little boy twisted his sled and in another second shot off the mound through the air. He landed well ahead of the others and whizzed to the bottom of the hill—the winner!

"He really did win!" Charlie shouted in surprise.

"He sure did! How did you get ahead of us, Freddie?" Bert asked.

His small brother told of zooming off the hump in the ground. "Great!" Bert praised him. "That was using your head!"

Freddie beamed, then he admitted, "I guess polishing the runners helped too!" He told Bert how he and Flossie had spent the morning. "We did yours and Nan's too," he added.

"Thanks, Freddie and Flossie," Bert said. "That was swell of you. Is that your surprise?"

The small twins nodded, delighted that their work was appreciated.

When Charlie and the Bobbseys reached the top of the hill again with their sleds they found that Danny Rugg, Jack Westley, and several older boys had arrived.

"Yah!" Danny jeered. "You're some coasters! We were watching. You let your little brother beat you!"

"All right," Bert replied in an even tone, "let's see *you* beat *me!*"

"Okay. That should be easy!" Danny blustered. "Are you ready?"

Without waiting for Bert's reply, the bully ran a few steps and threw himself on his sled. By the time the startled Bobbsey boy could get started, Danny was already several feet down the hill.

"That's not fair!" Nan cried indignantly. "He didn't give Bert any warning. They should have started at the same time!"

"Don't worry, Nan," Freddie said. "Remember I fixed the runners on Bert's sled. He can go faster than Danny!"

The race, however, appeared to be very even. At first Danny was ahead, then Bert caught up with him. Danny gave a little hunch which made his sled pick up speed.

"Come on, Bert!" Flossie shrieked.

"Look at that!" Freddie yelled.

Bert's sled had sped past Danny's and now fairly flew down the hill. In spite of the bully's desperate efforts, Bert reached the bottom of the hill a sled's length ahead of him.

Charlie and the other Bobbseys rushed up to congratulate Bert when he and Danny reached the top of the hill again. Danny was mad. He never liked to lose.

Jack walked over to his pal. "It wasn't a fair race," he said. "I heard Freddie Bobbsey say that he had fixed the runners on Bert's sled."

"Is that so?" Danny advanced on Bert with clenched fists. "I ought to sock you for that!"

"Now, Danny, who are you to talk?" Bert replied, standing his ground. "There was nothing unfair about the race, except that you started ahead of me."

"Jack says your runners were fixed!" Danny insisted.

Bert laughed. "Freddie fixed the rust on them. He sandpapered the runners clean. I guess there's no law against that!"

"All right then. I'll trade sleds with you," the bully proposed.

"Not on your life!" Bert exclaimed. "Your sled's all dirty and rusty. You never take care of anything!"

"You give me your sled, Bert Bobbsey,"

Danny threatened, "or I'll tell your mother and father your silly secret!"

Bert looked dashed. "Please don't do that, Danny. We want it to be a surprise at Christmas."

"Swap sleds with me then!"

At this point Nan spoke up. "Don't do it, Bert!" she said firmly. "I'm sure Danny doesn't know what our secret is!"

CHAPTER XII

CASTLE BUILDERS

"IS THAT so?" Danny sneered. "Well, *you'll* find out, Nan Bobbsey, that I know your Christmas secret!" With that he stalked away, his pal Jack close behind him.

The fear that Danny would reveal *Project Santa Claus* worried all the twins for the next two days. But nothing more was heard from the bully.

Early Monday morning Nan went into Mr. Tetlow's office. She asked the secretary if she might speak to the principal. In a few minutes the kindly man came to the door of his private office.

"Come in, Nan," he called. "What can I do for you?"

Nan asked permission for the Bobbseys to build the snow sculpture on the school lawn. "If we should happen to win the prize, we'd like to

donate the money to the school Library Fund,"
she added.

"That's very nice of you, Nan," Mr. Tetlow
replied. "I must say I have always found the
Bobbsey twins to be fine school citizens. It's a
good idea for the school to be represented in this
contest and I'm glad to appoint the Bobbsey
twins as official builders of the exhibit!"

"Thank you, Mr. Tetlow," Nan said as she
rose to leave. Then she hesitated. "Would it be
all right if we also used the snow castle for something else?" she asked.

"Use it?" Mr. Tetlow repeated. "How?"

Quickly Nan told him of the twins' *Project
Santa Claus.* "So you see, we'd like to have the
castle in it," she ended.

"Excellent!" Mr. Tetlow said with enthusi-
asm. "I think it's a splendid idea. Of course you
may use the snow sculpture!"

On the way home to lunch Nan told the other
twins of her talk with the principal.

"That's great, Nan!" Bert cried. "If Dad can
come up to help, let's start this afternoon!"

When the subject was brought up at the
luncheon table, Mr. Bobbsey looked uncertain.
"I'll try to make it," he said, "but this will be a
busy afternoon for me. If your mother and I

aren't at the school by four o'clock, you'd better come on home and we'll plan it for tomorrow."

The twins looked at one another and grinned. They needed an hour that afternoon to work on their secret project and had been wondering how to arrange it.

"This is perfect!" Bert declared on the way back to school that afternoon. "We can almost finish the surprise before Dad and Mother get there."

As soon as classes were over the twins and Nellie, with Charlie on guard, began their work in the big classroom. There was no sign of Danny and everything went smoothly.

Finally, a little before four o'clock, Nellie and Charlie left, and the twins, bundled in their heavy clothes, waited in front of the school.

After a few minutes Freddie asked anxiously, "Do you think Dad and Mommy are coming? It must be awful late!"

"Let's wait a little while longer," Nan proposed, "and then if they don't show up we'll go on home."

Freddie and Flossie began chasing each other around the school yard to keep warm while Bert and Nan swung their arms and stamped their feet. Just when the children had about given up, the Bobbsey station wagon stopped at the school gate and Mr. and Mrs. Bobbsey got out. They were dressed in ski clothes.

"Hi!" Mr. Bobbsey waved. "The sculptors are ready for work!"

"Goody!" Flossie exclaimed, running up and throwing her arms around her father. "How do we begin?"

"I'd say the first thing is to decide where to put the castle," Mr. Bobbsey replied.

"Why not build it at the front of the school lawn," Nan suggested. "Then everyone can see it."

Everyone agreed and they all began to stomp down the snow. Where the area was fairly level, Mr. Bobbsey drew the plan of the castle from his pocket. He and Bert studied the measurements—ten feet long and six feet deep.

"Let's get busy and make a supply of snowballs about a foot in diameter," Mr. Bobbsey suggested.

Gleefully Freddie and Flossie set about rolling snow into huge balls. Several times in their excitement they bumped into each other and sat down abruptly in the soft snow.

Bert and Nan worked quickly as well as Mr. and Mrs. Bobbsey. In half an hour they had a large pile of snowballs.

"I think that should do for a while," Mr. Bobbsey said. "Let's start the walls."

"Suppose you and Mother each take one," Nan suggested. "Freddie and I will work on a third and Flossie and Bert can build the fourth."

"Sure, and let's have a race," Freddie proposed.

Once more the Bobbseys set to work. On four sides of the tamped down area they pushed the snowballs close together into long lines. When the balls were used up, more were rolled. Soon it was too high for the small twins to be able to help lift the balls into place.

"Let's play inside the castle," Freddie suggested.

The two children climbed over and began to play tag. Then once when a large snowball fell inside and smashed, they put it together again.

By hard pushing they rolled the ball up the wall and heaved it into place.

"Wow! That was a job!" Freddie panted.

Half an hour later the walls were the right height of five and a half feet.

"That looks keen!" Bert exclaimed, and his family agreed.

By this time it was growing dark and the twins' hands were like ice.

Mr. Bobbsey straightened up with a groan. "I'm stiff!" he exclaimed, "and I'm sure the rest of you are tired. I suggest we call it a day and put on the towers tomorrow."

Everybody agreed, but suddenly Flossie cried, "We can't get out! There isn't any door!"

The others looked at one another in consternation. Then they burst out laughing. They had built the walls of the castle around the small twins!

"Get us out!" Flossie wailed.

Bert and his parents tried to scale the wall, but they could not climb the straight-set snow-balls.

"I know what!" Freddie exclaimed. "We can make a doorway!"

"Sure!" Bert agreed. "The old castles had high entranceways so the knights could ride into the courtyard on their horses!"

"We haven't anything to dig with," Nan said.

"There's a shovel in the station wagon," Mr. Bobbsey said. "Bert, get it."

When Bert returned with the tool, he started hacking into the center of the front wall. It was hard work, because the snow had already begun to freeze in the evening air. But Bert persisted and presently he had made an opening about two feet high and a foot wide.

"Try it!" Nan called through.

Triumphantly Freddie and Flossie crawled outside the castle!

"I'm glad we could get you out and not spoil the castle," Bert observed thankfully. "Tomorrow we'll make a regular doorway."

Mr. Bobbsey hugged the small twins, then said, "Dinah will be wondering where we are. Pile in the car, children."

The cook was watching for the headlights of

the station wagon and rushed to open the kitchen door as Mr. Bobbsey stopped in the driveway.

"Come in and get warm," Dinah urged. "You all look frozen. When you're ready I've got some nice stewed chicken and hot biscuits for you."

"Oh, that sounds marvelous!" Nan called as she took off her boots. Then she and Flossie ran upstairs to wash their hands.

In a short while the Bobbseys assembled at the dinner table. The tender chicken and light, flaky biscuits tasted good and were a perfect reward for an afternoon's hard work.

When Dinah had removed the dinner plates and came back into the dining room with the dessert, Freddie looked up. "Oh boy!" he exclaimed. The cook was carrying a big cake with shiny chocolate icing!

"That cake's a picture, Dinah," said Mrs. Bobbsey.

The jolly cook chuckled. "I figured if you all were goin' to build a whole castle, you'd be mighty hungry when you came home!" she said.

Later that evening when Mr. and Mrs. Bobbsey had gone out to visit friends and the small twins had sleepily tumbled into bed, Bert and Nan sat at the dining table and dug into their homework. For a while there was deep silence as they concentrated on the lessons for the next day.

Presently Nan sighed, put down her pencil, and looked up. "Have you finished your history assignment?" she asked her brother.

"Yes. Just this minute. Why?"

"Will you help me with my arithmetic? I can't seem to work out some of these problems. They're real puzzlers."

"Sure. Let's see them."

The two bent intently over Nan's book while Bert explained the solutions to the troublesome problems. Suddenly he stopped talking in the middle of a sentence and raised his head as if he were listening intently to something.

Nan looked at him curiously. "What's the matter?" she asked.

"Sh! Listen!"

"I don't hear anything," she remarked after a moment.

"I heard a strange sound," Bert explained, frowning. "There it is again. Did you hear it this time?"

"Yes." Nan cocked her head. "It seems to be coming from the street—sounds like a peculiar sort of whistle," she added thoughtfully. "I wonder who's doing it."

"Let's see if someone's out there," Bert proposed eagerly, pushing his chair from the table.

The two children ran to the front door and opened it. Once again they heard the strange whistle. Bert and Nan peered in every direction. But no one was in sight!

CHAPTER XIII

THE SURPRISE GUARD

"THAT'S queer," Nan observed. "The sound seemed to be so near and now there's no one around."

"It might have been a signal," Bert mused. Then he shrugged. "Well, no one's here now. I'm going to bed."

The next morning when the Bobbseys reached school they saw a crowd around their snow castle. As they came up, the group parted. Word had spread that it was the Bobbseys who had built it.

"Oh!" Flossie cried. "Our bee-yoo-ti-ful castle is ruined!"

The others gasped. Half the row of snowballs forming the front wall had been knocked off and deep gashes made in it.

"That's a crime!" one girl exclaimed angrily. "Who could have done it?"

"And look at the fire!" Freddie suddenly yelled. He had run to the rear and caught sight of a small bonfire burning close to the wall of the castle.

Quickly Bert dashed around to the back and kicked the fire apart. Then he smothered the glowing embers with snow.

"They nearly melted our castle!" Flossie wailed.

Bert examined all the walls. There was a slight sprinkling of new-fallen snow on them.

"Who do you think spoiled our castle, Bert?" Nan asked.

"I don't know, but I have an idea two people were responsible," he replied. "The hacking must have been done last night before the snow came down."

"But the bonfire couldn't have been set then," Nan said.

"Somebody built it just before school!" Freddie declared. "And if I'd just been here with my fire engine, I'd have put out that old fire and it wouldn't have melted the castle at all!"

Bert turned to the crowd of boys and girls.

"Did any of you see a person around here?" he asked.

"I did," a little boy spoke up. "Not close up, though. He had on a red hat."

Just then Danny and Jack joined the group. Danny was wearing a red ski cap! "What's the big commotion?" he asked casually. Jack looked unconcerned.

"As if you didn't know!" Bert cried. "You tried to ruin this castle just to get even with me because I won our race the other day!"

"I did not! You're always blaming me for everything, Bert Bobbsey," Danny replied, and stalked away, followed by his pal.

Just then the bell rang and the children trooped into the school. During Assembly Mr. Tetlow announced his permission for the Bobbseys to build their snow castle on the school grounds.

"If it receives a prize, the money will go to our school. For this reason it is doubly regrettable that vandals have tried to destroy it. I suggest that as many of you as possible help to repair the damage during recess."

There was loud applause. As a result, Bert and Nan had more help than they could use. Besides mending the wall, the children erected two of the four towers.

As the bell rang, Bert and Nan called out. "Oh, thanks loads, everybody!"

At the Bobbsey luncheon table the twins told their parents about the attack on the snow castle, and how their classmates had helped them to repair it.

"But we still have two towers to put on the rear corners," Nan said.

"Don't worry about it," Mr. Bobbsey replied. "I won't be able to help this afternoon, but we can all go over to the school early tomorrow morning and finish the job before the Christmas program begins."

There were to be no classes at the school the next morning; only the Christmas exercises, the children told him.

On their way back to school after lunch it was decided that Bert and Nan should make another trip to Mr. Holman's office that afternoon. It was in connection with their *Project Santa Claus.*

They met promptly after classes were over and set out on the errand. Half an hour later they rode up in the elevator to Mr. Holman's office.

"What's that on Mr. Holman's door?" Bert asked his twin as the elevator closed behind them.

"Oh dear!" Nan cried. "What will we do?"

The two children found a notice fastened to the glass. It read:

CLOSED FOR 8 DAYS

"Oh dear!" Nan cried. "What will we do? This means he won't be here again until after Christmas!"

Bert looked worried. "We'll have to get in touch with him some way. I'm sure he understood this was a Christmas project!"

"Maybe we can telephone him," Nan suggested.

Her twin agreed and the two children stopped at the public telephone booth in the lobby of the building. Bert looked up Mr. Holman's home address in the book.

"He lives on Maple Avenue," Bert reported. "That's on our way home. Let's stop and talk to him."

"But he may not be there," Nan said.

"Let's see anyway," Bert urged.

When they reached the man's house on Maple Avenue, Mr. Holman was just getting out of his car. "Hello there, Bobbsey twins!" he called jovially. "Did you think I had deserted you? Some important business came up that had to be taken care of immediately, so I closed the office today."

"But the sign said you'd be closed for *eight* days!" Nan said in surprise.

"Eight days!" Mr. Holman exclaimed. "When I put the sign up it said one!"

"Somebody must have changed it for a joke," Bert remarked.

"Well, come on in and we'll discuss this project of yours," the man suggested.

Bert and Nan explained about the damage to the snow castle and their plan to finish building it the next morning.

"After lunch tomorrow," Nan concluded, "we'll go back to school and finish the project."

"Fine! Fine!" Mr. Holman agreed. "Don't worry. Everything will be all right."

The twins said good-by and left. When they reached home Freddie and Flossie were waiting anxiously to hear the result of their interview with Mr. Holman.

Mrs. Bobbsey was entertaining a caller in the living room, and Dinah was making cookies, so the twins went up to the playroom on the third floor.

"Tell us quickly, Nan!" Flossie begged. "What did Mr. Holman say?"

Bert and Nan told of their surprise at finding the sign on the office door and Mr. Holman's explanation.

Freddie broke in. "I'll bet Danny did that! Remember, his father's office is in that building!"

"I think you're right, Freddie," Bert agreed. "Danny is doing everything he can to upset our plans!"

"But he didn't succeed this time!" Nan said. She told the small twins of the plan to return to school the next day to finish *Project Santa Claus* and Mr. Holman's assurance that everything would be all right.

"That's wonderful!" Flossie danced around the room. "Just think, in three more days it will be Christmas and Mother and Daddy will have our surprise!"

Bert had been quiet. Now he suddenly snapped his fingers. "I have an idea!" he exclaimed. "And I'll bet I'm right!"

"What do you mean?" Nan asked.

"You remember last night when we heard that funny whistle?"

"Yes."

"I thought then it might be a signal, and I'm sure it was—the signal to destroy our snow castle!"

"Oh, Bert!" Flossie exclaimed. "What are you talking about?"

"I'm not saying anything more now," Bert remarked mysteriously, "but I'm going to follow a certain hunch. I'll let you know if I'm right."

Although the twins begged him, Bert refused to discuss his statement any more. Directly after dinner Bert got ready to go out. "I have something to do. I'll see you at rehearsal, Nan." His sister looked puzzled, but she nodded in agreement.

When he left the house Bert hurried down the street until he came to the Rugg house. He could see Danny standing in the brightly lighted front hall.

"I'll just go to the side of the house," Bert told himself. "It's away from the light and no one will see me there."

He found a spot in the shrubbery where he could stand and be hidden from both the street and the house. Presently a boy came walking down the street. He stopped in front of Danny's house.

"Jack Westley!" Bert breathed triumphantly.

Jack looked up and down the street and then whistled in a strange fashion. It was the same sound Bert had heard the night before!

"I'm sure I'm right," Bert thought. "Jack

signaled for Danny last night and then they both went over to the school and wrecked our castle!"

In a moment he heard the whistle again from the porch of the house. He peered from his hiding place just far enough to see Danny come down the path and join Jack. The two boys walked away.

Bert waited until they were out of sight, then left his hiding place and followed them. They headed directly for Lakeport School!

"Boy, if they start wrecking the castle again, I can't fight both of them!" Bert thought in alarm. "I should have stopped for Charlie."

It was too late now. Bert hurried along after the bullies. When they turned around to see if anybody was watching them, Bert ducked behind a tree. The two boys continued on and in a few moments turned into the school playground.

As they disappeared back of the castle wall, Bert started to run. "You'll set no more fires to melt our sculpture, Danny and Jack!" he determined.

At this moment he heard a voice say, "What are *you* doin' here?"

"That voice sounds awfully familiar," Bert thought.

He peered around the corner of the wall. It was Sam Johnson!

"Now you scat and go home!" he ordered the two boys.

Danny and Jack were completely taken off guard. Finally Danny found his voice. "You can't order us around!" he blustered.

"I'm not orderin' you. I'm just telling you what's best for you," Sam said firmly.

Danny grunted. "I suppose Bert put you up to this," he taunted. "Bert's chicken—he's afraid to fight his own battles!"

"Is that so?" cried Bert, running up.

For the second time the two bullies were stunned. They gaped at Bert, who was advancing ready to fight if necessary.

Finally Danny said, "How many more have you got in hiding?"

Bert started to laugh. Sam chuckled. Danny and Jack, with sour faces, hurried away. Bert and Sam did not speak until the bullies were far up the street.

Then Bert said, "Thanks, Sam. You sure saved our castle! How did you happen to be here?"

Sam said he had decided to guard the snowball walls, because he "felt it in his bones" that someone might tamper with them again. "I'd

sure like to see you win that sculpture prize,"
he ended.

The kind man insisted upon staying on as
guard for a few more hours—at least until he
was sure Danny and Jack would be asleep. "And
I'll be back at six o'clock tomorrow morning,"
he added. "Now you run along home, Bert, and
don't worry any more."

"All right, Sam, and thanks again." Bert
shook the man's hand.

On the way home Bert's face wore a broad
grin. Danny Rugg had been outwitted!

CHAPTER XIV

BOO! BAH! BEAR!

THE NEXT morning the Bobbsey family was up early. Immediately after breakfast Mr. Bobbsey drove them over to the school. They set to work and in a little while had made a large collection of snowballs.

Freddie and Flossie were careful to stay outside the castle this time! They rolled the balls to each corner of the sculpture while Bert, Nan, and their parents put them in place for towers.

"We're making good progress," Bert said with satisfaction as he began to work on the fourth tower.

When they were in place, the family stood back to admire the effect.

"I think it looks very fine," Mr. Bobbsey remarked enthusiastically. "Now we'll enlarge the doorway and everything will be ready."

"I have something else!" Flossie cried. She

ran to the station wagon and returned with a small American flag. "I kept this from the Fourth of July," she explained. "Wouldn't it look nice on one of the towers?"

"Of course it would!" Nan exclaimed. "It's just the thing!"

Flossie beamed proudly as Bert stuck the flag in the front tower on the left-hand side.

"Now it's an American castle," Mrs. Bobbsey said as she pulled off her heavy gloves. "And we have time enough to go home and change our clothes before the Christmas program."

"One thing more," Mr. Bobbsey said. He went into the school and in a minute was back with a bucket of water.

"That's a wonderful idea, Dad," Bert said. "The water will freeze and make the castle hold its shape. Is that it?"

"Right, son." Carefully Mr. Bobbsey poured the water over the turrets of the snow castle and then returned the bucket to the janitor.

The family drove home and in an hour were back at the school. Mr. and Mrs. Bobbsey went into the auditorium while the children hurried backstage, where all was bustle and confusion.

When Miss Burns, the smaller twins' teacher, saw them, she called them over. "Freddie and Flossie," she said, "would you do me a great favor?"

"Of course, Miss Burns," they chorused.

"You remember Susie Larker and Teddy Blake were to sing a funny song this morning?" the pretty young teacher asked.

The twins nodded.

"Well, Mrs. Larker called. Susie has a cold and won't be able to come out, and Teddy doesn't want to sing alone."

"That's too bad," Flossie said. "How can we help?"

"Some of the children have told me that you and Freddie can sing a funny song—about a bear," the teacher replied. "I thought perhaps you'd sing it for us this morning."

The Bear Song was one that the small twins had learned recently. Freddie loved to sing it because in one part he could growl like a bear.

"I—I don't know—" Flossie began hesitantly.

"Sure we can!" Freddie interrupted.

Miss Burns smiled. "That's wonderful!" she said. "You'll go on right after the Senior Chorus."

Since Bert and Nan were members of the chorus, they had already taken their places on the stage. The group sang several Christmas carols and then marched off the platform. Nan was the last in line and as she stepped into the wings, the small twins passed her on their way to the stage.

"Flossie!" Nan whispered in surprise. "Where are you going?"

Flossie gave her sister an impish grin and the little twins ran on. The next moment Nan heard the familiar notes of the accompaniment to the Bear Song.

Freddie and Flossie walked to the center of the stage, bowed, and began to sing with gestures:

"The old, black bear came out of his den,
Boo! Bah!
Boo! Bah!
And what do you think the bear did then?
Boo! Bah!
Boo! Bah!
He wiggled his head,
He waggled his tail,
He scratched his nose,
He twiddled his toes.
And what did the funny old bear do then?
Why, he went back and hid in his den.
Boo! Bah! Boo! Bah!
Boooo-oo-oo—oo!"

The audience roared at Freddie's growls and the acting that accompanied the words of the song. They applauded wildly.

Encouraged by their reception, Freddie and Flossie sang the second verse.

"The old, black bear climbed up a tree,

"Boo! Bah! Boo! Bah!"
sang the twins

Boo! Bah!
Boo! Bah!
And what do you think he climbed to see?
Boo! Bah!
Boo! Bah!
He opened his eyes,
He stuck out his tongue,
He sat on a branch,
He nibbled a bun,
But what did the funny old black bear see?
Why, before he could look he was stung by a
bee.
And then he fell *bump!* down out of the tree.
Boo! Bah! Boo! Bah!
Boo-oo-oo—oo!"

Freddie and Flossie were followed by the
Junior Chorus, which sang more Christmas
music. That ended the program.

When the Bobbsey children met their parents
afterward, Mrs. Bobbsey exclaimed, "Freddie
and Flossie, why didn't you tell us you were
going to sing? We were so surprised when you
came out onto the stage!"

Nan laughed. "So were Bert and I. We didn't
know anything about it."

"It was a last minute s'prise for everyone,"
Flossie explained, then she told about Susie's
cold.

Back at home, Dinah threw up her hands when Freddie told her about singing the Bear Song. "Well, honey child," she exclaimed, "I'm sure proud of you and Flossie. You're real good singers!"

After lunch the twins announced that they were going downtown. "We have to buy gifts for Dinah and Sam," Nan whispered to her mother in explanation.

They went first to the school and there in a short while completed their *Project Santa Claus*. Then they walked down to the center of town to do their shopping.

"I'm sure glad we received our allowances this morning," said Flossie, heaving a sigh of relief. "Freddie and I spent our very last cent when we went Christmas shopping last Saturday."

"You sound very mysterious, Flossie," Nan replied. "Did *I* happen to be involved in your shopping spree?" she asked mischievously.

"Well, partly," Flossie answered slowly. "I can't tell you any more now. But just remember that I said 'our very last cent!' "

Nan laughed. Then the twins entered the department store.

"What shall we get for Dinah?" Flossie asked as they walked down an aisle. She paused at a counter which displayed bright-colored strings of beads. "Do you think she'd like these?"

"She might," Nan agreed.

"You and Flossie pick out Dinah's present," Bert proposed, "and Freddie and I will choose something for Sam."

"Okay. Flossie and I will meet you back here in a little while."

The twins separated. Nan and Flossie strolled about and finally selected a pretty red-and-white printed blouse for Dinah. "I think she will look nice in this when she goes out with Sam," Flossie remarked.

The girls met Bert and Freddie, and admired the leather belt which the boys had bought for Sam. "I heard Sam tell Dinah he needed a new belt," Freddie informed them.

"I have money enough to treat everyone to ice cream," Nan announced. "Let's go to the soda fountain here."

"Oh yummy, yes," said Flossie.

The twins were soon enjoying large dishes of their favorite flavors. Then they came out onto the street.

"It's beginning to snow again!" Bert exclaimed. "We'd better hurry home."

The children had walked only a short distance before they realized that the wind was blowing very hard. It whipped the stinging snow against their faces. Bert and Nan walked in front of the small twins to keep some of the blast from them.

"This is fun!" Freddie exclaimed, but the wind carried his words away as soon as they were out of his mouth.

As the children trudged on, the wind grew fiercer. They were hardly able to see the walk in front of them, and stumbled frequently. It was beginning to grow dark and the small twins were nearly exhausted.

"Maybe we should have taken a taxi," Nan remarked as she turned to help Flossie, who had slipped into a small drift.

"I guess it would've been better," Bert agreed. "But there aren't any taxis around here." He looked up the deserted street.

"Where are we?" Nan asked. "The snow is blowing in my eyes so hard I can't see!"

Bert peered up at a street sign as they came to a corner. "We're on Hedden Place at the corner of Wright Avenue."

"Oh dear!" Nan groaned. "We're ten blocks from home!"

"They're short blocks," Bert said encouragingly. "I think we can make it."

So the children pushed on through the storm. Freddie kept hold of Flossie's hand and they

tried to follow in Bert's and Nan's footsteps.
Suddenly Flossie cried out and sat down in the
snow.

"What's the matter?" Nan asked in alarm,
turning around to help her little sister.

"I slipped," Flossie explained. "My feet are so
cold I can't feel them!"

"Bert," Nan exclaimed, "I think we should go
into the nearest house and call home. Daddy will
come for us!"

"I guess you're right," Bert agreed. "Let's go
in here."

At that moment the wind was blowing the
snow so hard that the children could hardly see
the house they were approaching. But as they
struggled up the walk, Freddie exclaimed,
"Why we're at Aunt Sally Pry's!"

"So we are!" Nan cried. "Aren't we lucky?"
She rang the doorbell and in a moment Mrs.
Pry opened the door.

"Well, goodness gracious," she exclaimed, "if
it isn't the Bobbsey twins! What are you doing
out in this storm? Come in! Come in!"

She closed the door behind them, then led the
way into the living room where a wood fire was
crackling merrily.

"Ooh, how wonderful!" Flossie ran to the

fire and stretched out her mittened hands to the warmth.

"Where have you been?" Aunt Sally asked. "You shouldn't be out in this storm."

"We've been to the store," Freddie explained.

"You knocked at the door?" she asked. "I'm sorry I didn't hear you."

"No, no," Nan put in, smiling at the dear old lady. "We've been to the store to do some shopping. We were on our way home when the storm started."

"May we use your telephone to call Dad?" Bert asked.

"Of course, my dears," Aunt Sally said. "And you must wait right here by the fire until he comes for you."

Mr. and Mrs. Bobbsey were relieved to hear that the children had found shelter and promised to drive over for them at once.

Suddenly Nan exclaimed, "Oh, do you suppose this storm will ruin our snow castle?"

Bert looked grim as he replied, "There's a good possibility it will, Nan!"

CHAPTER XV

DRUMMERS

ALL THE twins worried about their snow castle. Would the storm ruin it? When they awoke the next morning the thought was still in their minds.

"Let's go over to school and look at it," Nan proposed, as the family sat at the breakfast table enjoying Dinah's golden pancakes and crisp slices of bacon.

"Perhaps you'd better," Mr. Bobbsey agreed. "I must get down to the lumberyard early, so I can't go with you. If the wall has been damaged, see if you can fix it up. The Town Committee will be inspecting all the entries this afternoon."

"When will they announce the winner?" Flossie asked eagerly.

"This evening at the Tree Lighting ceremony in front of the Town Hall," Mr. Bobbsey replied.

"And tomorrow is Christmas!" Freddie exclaimed. "Hurray!"

"Hurry over and look at the castle," Mrs. Bobbsey suggested, "and then come back. There's lots of shoveling to do."

When the twins were ready to leave they found Snap sitting by the front door. At their approach he got up with a little whine, wagging his tail eagerly.

"Let's take him with us," Flossie proposed. "He wants to see our castle!"

"All right," Bert agreed. "But get his leash, Freddie. We'll have to keep him out of the snowbanks."

Freedie ran off and returned in a few minutes. He had hung three tinkling Christmas bells on the dog's leash.

"Snap is a Christmas reindeer!" he announced, as he fastened the leash to the dog's collar.

Flossie giggled appreciatively. Snap trotted off briskly, pulling Freddie behind him.

Nan ran ahead as they reached the school grounds. "Our castle is all covered up!" she exclaimed in dismay.

Bert joined his twin. "This is just loose snow," he said, brushing some of it away. "I think we can get it off without damaging our sculpture."

He was right. The castle had frozen into a solid block of ice-covered snow and the recent storm had left only a top layer of the soft white stuff.

The twins set to work busily and with the aid of scarves and mittens they dusted off the top of the four walls and the towers. The flag flapped in the breeze, its stick having frozen solid to the tower.

Freddie held Snap's leash with difficulty, for the dog was jumping around restlessly. "Sit still!" Freddie begged the pet.

But Snap did not mind. Suddenly he darted past Nan, who was standing next to Freddie. Then, reaching the end of the leash, he turned and started back again. This wound the leather around Nan's ankles. She lost her balance and fell against the icy castle!

As she slid to the ground Nan's head scraped a sharp corner of the snow sculpture. She lay still!

"Oh, Nan!" Freddie cried as he ran to her side. "Are you hurt?"

Bert and Flossie hurried from the other side of the castle where they had been working. As

Snap's leash wound around Nan's ankles

Bert bent over his sister, she opened her eyes and sat up.

When Nan saw his worried face, she grinned and murmured, "I'm all right. What happened?"

"Snap upset you," Freddie exclaimed. "I guess he got tired of being on a leash."

"You have a mean scratch on your forehead," Bert observed. "I think we'd better go home and let Mother fix it."

He helped Nan to her feet and the four children started home. When they reached it and Mrs. Bobbsey saw Nan's head, she exclaimed, "Bert, bring me the First Aid kit right away, please."

After she had applied antiseptic and a plastic bandage to the long red scratch, Nan described the mishap.

"Snap didn't mean to upset you," Freddie said when the others had finished their tale. "I know he's sorry, Nan."

Nan smiled and hugged her little brother. "I'm not angry at Snap," she assured him. "I know he was just feeling frisky."

"Do you feel well enough to help with the Christmas decorations, Nan?" Mrs. Bobbsey asked. "Perhaps you should lie down for a while."

"I feel fine, Mother. I'd like to help," Nan protested.

"All right, then. Suppose you and Bert decorate the mantelpiece in the living room. Sam left a pile of greens by the back door."

"What can Freddie and I do?" Flossie piped up.

"Dinah has popped some corn and there are cranberries in the kitchen. You and Freddie can string them for the tree."

In a few minutes the small twins were seated at the kitchen table busily threading popcorn and cranberries into long chains. Dinah bustled about, getting food ready for the Christmas dinner next day.

Bert and Nan carried armloads of pine branches into the living room and began to arrange them on the mantel. Finally Nan stood back to study the arrangement.

"I think it needs something else," she said.

"Like what?"

"Do you remember those little figures we had at our Christmas party last year? They'd be very good. I'll go and ask Mother where they are."

In a few minutes Nan returned to the room carrying a pasteboard carton. She and Bert unpacked the tiny figures, which Nan arranged in a procession on the edge of the mantel in front of the greens. There were musicians dressed in red, one playing a flute, one a violin, and one a drum. Then came a sleigh pulled by six tiny, prancing horses.

Bert meanwhile had found other figurines of pixies and elves dressed in bright red and green. These were stuck among the fragrant pine needles.

Freddie and Flossie ran into the room to see how the decorations were coming along. "Oh, how bee-yoo-ti-ful!" Flossie exclaimed, gazing wide-eyed at the mantel.

"That looks great!" Freddie agreed.

Bert went for a stepladder and fastened a small sprig of mistletoe over each doorway, while Nan set vases of green branches on two tables.

"The room looks lovely, children," Mrs. Bobbsey exclaimed when she came in.

Later, as they were finishing luncheon, the Bobbseys heard the sound of drums. Flossie jumped up and raced to the window.

"It's a parade!" she cried. "Let's follow it!"

By this time all the family had gathered at the window. They saw three young boys with bright red scarves around their necks. One was pushing an enormous drum while the others took turns beating it. On the drum in big black letters was:

LAKEPORT SNOW-SCULPTURE CONTEST

Mr. Bobbsey chuckled. "Those three men behind the boys are the committee," he said. "They're really doing their job in a big way!"

"May we follow them, Daddy?" Freddie begged. "They must be going around to look at all the statues!"

Mr. and Mrs. Bobbsey gave their permission and the twins rushed to put on their heavy snow clothes. In a few minutes the children caught up with the small group which was already following the judges.

The little procession went up one street and down another, stopping at every piece of snow sculpture. The committee of three men carefully examined each statue and made marks in their notebooks.

Presently they reached Nellie Parks' home. On the lawn were two snow figures. One had a small waist and a flowing skirt, while the other had a knee-length coat and a crown on his head. The man's figure held a tiny slipper on his outstretched hand.

"Cinderella and the Prince!" Flossie exclaimed. "I know it is!"

Nellie had run out of her house when the group stopped. "You've guessed it, Flossie!" she cried. "I hope the judges did too!"

One of the men heard her. "An excellent entry, young lady," he said. "It shows a good deal of imagination and is very well done." He made a note in his book before he turned away to join the others.

"Maybe Nellie will win the prize," Flossie whispered to Nan.

"Come on!" Bert called to them. "The parade has stopped again!"

The twins waved good-by to Nellie and ran down the street. The committee had paused before another sculpture in front of Teddy Blake's house. This one looked like a little girl with a long cape. On one arm she carried a basket. Standing next to her was what appeared to be a large dog.

"Little Red Riding Hood!" Freddie shouted. "And that's the wolf! See, his big, red tongue is hanging out!"

The crowd laughed at Freddie's excitement. The three men walked around the figures, examining them carefully. They seemed to be very much impressed. Teddy had come outside and was watching the men excitedly.

The twins ran up to their little friend and

praised his snow statue. "I bet it'll win," Freddie declared.

Teddy was pleased at their admiration of his work. "I sure feel like I'm on pins and needles." He grinned.

"We do, too," Flossie admitted.

Teddy then asked if the judge had seen the Bobbseys' castle. Bert nodded.

"I think so," Bert replied. "I heard someone say the committee started in the school neighborhood."

All this while, the judges had been consulting in low voices. In a few moments, however, the committee moved on, with the boys once more announcing the parade by beating on the big drum. The Bobbseys waved good-by to Teddy and followed the procession, while more snow statues representing many subjects were reviewed.

Finally, having looked over the last sculpture, the three men stepped into a car which drove up. One of them leaned from the window before driving off and called, "See you all at the Tree-Lighting ceremony in the Town Square tonight. We'll make our announcement of the winner then!"

"Oh, I can't wait!" Freddie cried, jumping up and down. "Let's go home and have an early supper, so we can go to the ceremony right afterward."

"Bert and I want to go down to Mr. Holman's first," Nan told her small brother as the twins started back. "We won't be long. See you soon."

The small twins said good-by and hurried off. Back home once more, Freddie and Flossie helped their mother with little last-minute jobs in preparation for Christmas day. Mr. Bobbsey came home early, his arms full of gaily wrapped, different-sized packages.

"I'll put these in the hall closet," he said. "And remember, that closet is off limits to all Bobbsey twins!"

Freddie and Flossie giggled and Flossie exclaimed, "Oh, I'm so glad tomorrow is Christmas! I don't think I could wait another day!"

"Me either!" Freddie agreed. "I'm ready to burst!"

When the supper hour arrived Mrs. Bobbsey looked worried. "Bert and Nan aren't home yet," she said to the others. "They knew we were going to have supper early so we could get to the Tree-Lighting ceremony on time. I wonder what's taking them so long?"

CHAPTER XVI

"MERRY CHRISTMAS, DANNY!"

FREDDIE and Flossie also wondered why Bert and Nan had not returned home.

"I'm sure they'll be here soon," Flossie assured her mother.

"We'll wait another fifteen minutes," Mrs. Bobbsey decided. "If they're not here by then, we'll have supper. Dinah can keep their food warm for them. It's funny, though, they didn't phone."

In the meantime Bert and Nan were having a disturbing afternoon. When they reached the building where Mr. Holman had his office, they found a substitute elevator man on duty.

"Where's Dave?" Bert asked.

"He's off duty now. He's due back any moment. What floor do you want?"

"The fourth, please," Nan said politely.

A few seconds later the door opened and the twins stepped out. They walked over to Mr. Holman's office and tried the door. It was locked!

"Oh, Bert!" Nan groaned. "What do you suppose has happened now?"

"Mr. Holman must be here," Bert replied. "Maybe he just didn't want anybody else coming in, so he locked the door."

Bert knocked loudly several times but there was no answer. Mr. Holman had evidently left early. In despair the twins turned away and walked back to the elevator.

"What shall we do now?" Nan asked. "Go to Mr. Holman's house again?"

"Let's try telephoning him first," Bert suggested. "We can use the phone in the lobby."

When they reached the Holman number a woman answered. "No, he's not here," she said in reply to Nan's inquiry. Then she called, "Hold on a minute! He's just coming in."

In another second Nan was relieved to hear their friend's hearty voice. When she asked about *Project Santa Claus* he seemed puzzled. "Why, I left it with Dave, the elevator operator. He promised to be on the lookout for you and to deliver the package."

Nan explained that Dave was off duty. "We'll

wait for him and ask for the package. Thank you, Mr. Holman!"

"That's all right," the man replied. "Merry Christmas to the Bobbsey family!"

After Nan had hung up she explained the situation to Bert. The boy pressed the bell for the elevator again. "Maybe Dave's back now," he remarked.

Presently the elevator arrived and Dave was now at the control. He looked surprised to see Bert and Nan.

"Mr. Holman said he left a package for us with you," Bert said.

"Yes, he did," Dave replied, "but your friend picked it up. Too bad you came down for it, too!"

"Our friend! What friend?" Nan gasped.

"Why, that boy you were with the other day. You know, dark hair, a little stockier than you, Bert."

"Danny Rugg!" Bert exploded.

"Yes. I remember now. I *have* seen him with Mr. Rugg," the elevator man said.

"How did he know the package was here?" Nan asked.

Dave explained that he had placed the package addressed to the Bobbsey Twins on the elevator stool. "When this boy got in, he saw it and said you had sent him to pick it up. Shouldn't I have given it to him?" Dave asked with a worried look.

"That's all right. We'll get it back!" Bert replied grimly.

Nan spoke up. "You see, Danny thinks it's funny to play mean tricks on us. It isn't your fault."

The twins waved good-by to Dave as cheerfully as they could and started off toward the Rugg home. By now it was quite dark.

"Danny is certainly doing his best to spoil our Christmas secret," Nan said sadly.

"Yes. And I'm just about fed up with Mr. Danny Rugg!" Bert exclaimed, doubling up his fists.

In a little while the twins reached the Rugg home. Mrs. Rugg came to the door when Bert rang the bell.

"Do you want to see Danny?" she asked. "I think he's upstairs getting ready to go to the Tree-Lighting ceremony tonight."

"We're very anxious to see him, Mrs. Rugg," Nan ventured.

Mrs. Rugg went to the foot of the stairs. "Danny!" she called. "Bert and Nan Bobbsey are here and would like to see you."

"I can't come," was the reply from upstairs.

"It's really very important," Nan persisted.

"Danny, I want you to come down here at once," his mother replied in a firm tone.

"Oh! All right!" the bully said sullenly. A moment later he clattered down the stairs. "What do you want?" he blustered.

"We want the package you took from the elevator," Bert said.

"I didn't take any old package!"

Nan spoke up. "Yes, you did! Dave, the elevator man, told us you said you'd bring it to us. Where is it?" Danny was silent.

Mrs. Rugg had not left the hall. Now she turned to her son. "Danny, if you are holding something belonging to the Bobbseys, return it at once!"

The bully shifted from one foot to the other and hung his head. "I can't," he muttered. "I threw it away!"

"Oh, Danny! You didn't!" Nan wailed.

"Where did you throw it?" Bert demanded. "You must know that!"

Mrs. Rugg looked sternly at her son. "You'd better go out with the Bobbseys and find it right away! I don't know what makes you do these things!"

"Aw, they're always picking on me," Danny said defensively.

However, he put on his coat and snow boots and followed Bert and Nan out the door. Once on the sidewalk Danny turned in the direction of the school.

"Where did you throw the package?" Nan asked as they walked along.

"Can't you do anything but ask questions?" Danny replied rudely. "If you want the old package, I'll show you where I left it."

Finally, the three children arrived in front of the school.

"Your package is in there!" Danny cried,

pointing to the snow castle shining in the moon-
light. With that, he started to run away, but
Bert was too quick for him.

"No, you don't!" Bert exclaimed, grabbing
the bully's arm. "You'll stay here until we find
it!"

Reluctantly Danny allowed himself to be
pulled toward the front of the snow castle. Bert
and Nan stared in astonishment. The doorway
had been blocked up!

"Danny, did you do that?" Bert stormed.

The other boy remained silent, sure proof of
his guilt.

"You're just impossible!" Nan cried angrily.
"Get that carton, Danny Rugg. You're *not*
going to spoil our Christmas."

The bully did not move, until Bert, fists
clenched, advanced toward him. Finally Danny
broke down. "Okay. Help me over the wall and
I'll get it."

Nan broke in, "You ought to make a new
opening, too!"

"That's an idea," said Bert. "We'll combine
the two jobs. Well, Danny, get going!"

Sullenly, Danny went to the entrance he had
blocked up and began kicking at the snow to
loosen it. "Too icy," said Danny. After a moment he added, "I think I know where there's an

old baseball bat. Maybe that would help."

"Oh, yes! Hurry and get it!" said Nan.

The bully ran to the row of shrubbery which was planted across the front of the school building. Getting down on his knees, he searched the bushes and presently pulled out a well-worn baseball bat.

"I hope it works," Nan said when Danny returned.

With hard whacks the boy struck the frozen snow blocking the entrance. Bit by bit it loosened. Bert and Nan, using their hands as shovels, scooped up the icy pieces.

"How did you know that old bat was there?" Bert asked.

Danny looked embarrassed. "Oh, Jack and I were fooling around here one day and found it," he said.

Bert's eyes narrowed. "And you used it to damage our castle, didn't you?"

"Yes, we did, since you're so smart!" Danny answered defiantly.

"Did Jack build the fire that morning?" Nan asked.

"Sure. We thought that was a good joke, but you Bobbseys never think anything's funny!" Danny sneered.

"I suppose you also thought it was a good joke to change the sign on Mr. Holman's office door!" Bert observed.

Danny was obviously flustered. But he tried to cover it up by demanding loudly, "What do you mean? What sign?"

Nan explained about the changing of the numeral from "1" to "8" in the sign and what she and Bert had learned from their visit to Mr. Holman's home.

"So your trick really didn't work out the way you thought it would," she concluded.

"It was a good try, though!" Danny blurted out. "Bet I had you silly kids scared good for a while." Then he realized that by these remarks he had admitted playing the prank. His face turned beet red.

As Danny started to leave without saying a word, kind-hearted Nan called, "Merry Christmas, Danny!"

"Merry Christmas!" Bert added.

Finally, Danny, ashamed of his tricks, turned around and answered, "Merry Christmas." Then he ran off as fast as he could.

Without further delay Bert hurried inside the castle and picked up the *Project Santa Claus* carton. To his relief it appeared to be undamaged. As he and Nan rushed back toward their home, Nan looked up at a clock in a church tower and said worriedly:

"Oh, Bert, it's nearly seven o'clock. Do you think we'll be too late for the Tree-Lighting ceremony and the announcement of the snow-sculpture awards?"

CHAPTER XVII

PRIZE WINNERS

WHEN Bert and Nan walked into the dining room a short time later they were greeted by a chorus of questions.

"What happened?"

"Where have you been?"

Mrs. Bobbsey interrupted. "No more questions now. Let Bert and Nan eat their supper. We must leave in a few minutes for the Tree-Lighting ceremony."

But Bert could tell from the worried expressions on the faces of Freddie and Flossie that the small twins were wondering if anything had happened to spoil *Project Santa Claus*.

"We just want to report 'mission accomplished,' and that's all until tomorrow morning," he said with a grin.

161

Freddie and Flossie burst into relieved giggles and returned to their dessert of gingerbread and applesauce.

Mr. and Mrs. Bobbsey smiled at each other. "I'll certainly be glad to find out what this big secret is," Mr. Bobbsey said. "I haven't been able to eat or sleep lately just wondering about it!" This remark brought delighted laughs from Mrs. Bobbsey and the children.

When supper was over the family bundled into warm clothes and Mr. Bobbsey drove them to the Town Square for the Tree-Lighting ceremony. The giant tree stood in the center of the small park. It was decorated with huge plastic balls of different colors which swayed and danced in the evening breeze.

"It's bee-yoo-ti-ful!" Flossie exclaimed, her blue eyes shining as she looked at the tall Christmas tree.

The Lakeport residents who had gathered in the square stood quietly while Mayor Rankin gave a short address of welcome. Then they all joined in singing a Christmas carol.

When the last note was sung, the mayor said, "Citizens of Lakeport, I am sure you are all eager to learn the winner of the Lakeport Snow-Sculpture Contest. It gives me great pleasure to announce—"

At that moment there came a squeal from one side of the park and a sudden movement of the crowd. Freddie and Flossie Bobbsey, who had been standing on a bench in order to see the platform, had leaned too hard against the back. Over went the bench and the twins with it!

Quickly they picked themselves up and brushed the snow from their coats. "Are you all right?" Mr. Bobbsey asked.

"Ye-es, I guess so," Flossie replied doubtfully.

"Who won the contest?" Freddie put in eagerly.

"We don't know," their father said teasingly. "You drowned out the mayor's announcement!"

"Oh, Daddy! How awful!" Flossie said, her cheeks pink with embarrassment.

But now Mayor Rankin, observing that nothing serious had happened, resumed his speech. "As I said, it gives me great pleasure to announce that first prize goes to the entry in the name of Lakeport School!"

"That's ours!" Freddie cried.

The mayor smiled. "This entry is a medieval snow castle built by the Bobbsey family. The committee feels that it represents the greatest imagination and skill of all the entries." He continued, "I understand the prize money is to go to the school Library Fund."

Applause broke out. When it had died down, Mayor Rankin spoke again. "Will the Bobbsey family please come to the platform to receive the prize?"

Mr. and Mrs. Bobbsey smilingly declined, so Freddie, Flossie, Bert, and Nan walked up and accepted the check from the mayor. The crowd clapped heartily.

The official gave honorable mention to Nellie

Parks' *Cinderella* and Teddy Blake's *Little Red Riding Hood*. Then he held up his hand. "One more announcement. Since the Bobbseys won first price, the committee has decided it is fitting to give the twins the honor of lighting the tree!"

"Oh! Thank you, Mr. Mayor!" Freddie and Flossie exclaimed in a chorus.

A stepladder was brought and placed near the tree. Flossie and Freddie climbed up, with Bert and Nan holding the supports. The little girl and her twin reached among the branches to the electric switch.

"Click it!" Bert urged.

With the eyes of the townspeople turned on the children, Flossie and Freddie together pushed the switch.

The tree burst into light, amid cheers and applause! Now more carols were sung, then the crowd dispersed. Everyone could be heard calling "Merry Christmas!"

Later, when the Bobbseys were in their car on the way home, Nan said, "Oh, isn't Christmas Eve just the loveliest time of the year!"

"I like Christmas morning better when we get our presents," Freddie put in practically.

Early the next day Flossie opened her eyes to

see the sunshine streaming through the windows This was the long-awaited, exciting day! She jumped up and ran over to Nan's bed.

"Merry Christmas!" she shouted. "Wake up, Nan! It's Christmas!"

Nan sat up in bed and rubbed her eyes sleepily. "Merry Christmas!" she echoed.

"Come on! Let's wake Bert and Freddie!" Flossie suggested, her eyes dancing.

The two girls put on robes and slippers and tiptoed to the room which the boys shared. As Nan put her hand on the knob, the door was thrown open!

"Merry Christmas!" Freddie cried. He and Bert stood in pajamas laughing at their sisters.

All the rustling and opening and closing of doors had awakened Mr. and Mrs. Bobbsey. "What's going on out there?" Mr. Bobbsey called from their room.

"Merry Christmas!" four happy voices shouted in chorus.

"Oh, is it Christmas?" Mr. Bobbsey asked as if surprised.

The twins giggled, then Nan asked, "May we go downstairs and look at our presents?"

"Yes," Mrs. Bobbsey answered, "but you boys put on your robes and slippers. Your father and

I will be right down. Look at your stocking presents until we come."

The four children dashed down the stairs and into the living room. In one corner stood a beautiful tree glistening with tinsel and bright-colored ornaments as well as ropes of popcorn and cranberries.

The floor around the tree was piled with gaily wrapped boxes. From the mantelpiece hung four bright-red stockings bulging with little packages, and topped with grinning Santa Clauses.

Bert switched on the tree lights. Then, taking down their stockings, the twins sank happily to the floor and dumped out the contents. There were nuts in the toe of each stocking and at the top a beautiful golden orange. In between were all sorts of little toys.

"Look!" Freddie cried, holding up a fire engine not more than two inches long.

There was also a set of little plastic fire-fighters, a bag of marbles, and a small viewer with pictures of African animals.

"See my dolly!" Flossie exclaimed as she unwrapped a little baby doll dressed in a tiny snowsuit. "And a little kitchen!" she added, setting out a miniature range with tiny pots and pans. There was even a toy refrigerator with a door which opened.

Nan's stocking contained a fancy box of various colored pencils, an assortment of ribbons for her hair, and several puzzles.

"This is great!" Bert exclaimed as he examined a small pocket flashlight. He, too, had puzzles as well as an automatic pencil.

By the time the children had finished examining and exclaiming over the stocking contents, Mr. and Mrs. Bobbsey had come downstairs.

Then Dinah and Sam walked in. "Merry Christmas, everybody!" they called, and Dinah added, "Breakfast is ready."

"You may see your other presents after we've eaten," Mrs. Bobbsey explained in reply to dismayed cries from the children.

How good Dinah's golden waffles and crisp Virginia ham were! When Freddie had finished his last bite, he slipped from his chair.

"May I go back to the presents now, Mother?" he asked.

"Yes, we're all coming," Mrs. Bobbsey replied with a smile.

What a flurry of paper and ribbon there was as the children stripped the wrappings from the boxes!

"Wowee!" Freddie cried. "Here's that hook-and-ladder truck I saw in the store. Now I can be a real fireman!" He began to pull the apparatus around the room.

"And my bee-yoo-ti-ful doll, Miss Melody!" Flossie exclaimed, clasping it in her arms. "It's the same one I touched in the store. Listen!"

Gently she touched the hand of the golden-curled doll. "Hello, how are you?" a high voice responded. Flossie laughed in delight. "Isn't she wonderful?

"And see my sweater set!" Nan cried. She held up soft cherry-colored twin sweaters.

"Just the books I wanted!" Bert observed. He had been admiring a set of do-it-yourself books in the Lakeport bookstore all fall and here they were under the tree!

Nan declared that the little leather change purse which the small twins gave her was exactly the kind she liked. Bert began to put the model plane together at once. "This is really neat!" he exclaimed.

Freddie and Flossie smiled happily at each other. There were other gifts for everyone and then Dinah and Sam came in to receive their presents.

From behind her back Dinah produced four

gingerbread Santa Clauses. Their red coats were made of sugar icing and each one had a cherry for a nose.

"Oh Dinah, they're darling!" Nan cried as the cook gave each of the twins one.

"I got somethin' to go with them," Sam remarked, and from a paper bag he pulled four sets of tiny wooden reindeer. "I carved them myself," he said proudly.

"How clever, Sam!" Nan exclaimed. They all thanked the smiling man.

Then Flossie gave Dinah the box which she and Nan had wrapped in shining silver paper. When the cook opened it her eyes grew wide. "Well, I never!" she exclaimed in delight. She lifted the blouse from the paper and held it up to her shoulders. "How do I look, Sam?" she asked her husband.

Sam clapped his knee with his hand. "Dinah, you sure look beautiful!" he said. Then when Freddie presented him with the leather belt he beamed all over. "I'm goin' to look pretty good myself!" he cried.

After everyone had admired all the presents again, Nan gave Bert a meaningful look.

"Ahem," he said. Everybody looked at him. "We twins now wish to present to Mother and Dad our *Project Santa Claus!*"

CHAPTER XVIII

YOUNG ACTORS

MR. BOBBSEY stared at the package which Bert had given him. "What can it be?" he asked.

Flossie jumped up and down in excitement. "Open it, Daddy! Open it!" she cried.

"Will it jump out and bite me?" he asked.

"Oh, Daddy! Stop teasing!" the little girl begged.

Carefully her father unwrapped the box and then lifted the lid. "Why, it's a movie film!" he exclaimed, passing it over to Mrs. Bobbsey to look at.

"What is the picture, children?" she asked curiously.

The twins shook their heads. "You'll have to run it," Nan said.

"What are we waiting for then?" Mr. Bobbsey said briskly. "Bert, get the projector and screen while I set up a table. Mary, you, Dinah, Sam, and the children find chairs. The performance will begin shortly."

Bert ran from the room while the others settled themselves. He came back carrying the movie projector in one hand and the rolled screen under the other arm. In a few minutes Mr. Bobbsey had the film threaded through the projector and Bert had placed the screen in front of the fireplace.

"All set!" Mr. Bobbsey called. "Nan, maybe you'd better pull the curtains."

She did so, and the room was plunged into semi-darkness.

Light flickered on the screen, then came the words: THE MAGIC WAND by Nan Bobbsey.

"Oh Nan! How wonderful!" Mrs. Bobbsey exclaimed. "Your prize-winning play!"

Now the cast of characters appeared. It read:

The Prince..............Bert Bobbsey
The Princess.............Nan Bobbsey
The Little Prince.........Freddie Bobbsey
The Little Princess.......Flossie Bobbsey
The Wicked Witch.......Nellie Parks

There was a brief pause, then ACT ONE flashed on the screen. The colored scene which followed showed Bert and Nan strolling in the courtyard of the snow castle.

Nan wears a long, gold-colored dress, a flowing shoulder robe, and a sparkling crown on her dark hair. The prince, played by Bert, wears tight-fitting green-satin trousers, a white blouse, and long purple cape. He, too, has a crown.

"All the costumes came from Aunt Sally Pry's," Nan explained. "We made the crowns from cardboard, and covered them with beads she gave us."

"They look like real jewels," Mrs. Bobbsey remarked, watching the screen as a head topped with long white hair and a conical hat peered through the doorway of the snow castle.

"Nellie Parks!" Mr. Bobbsey chuckled.

"This is wonderful, children!" Mrs. Bobbsey cried. "How did you get the film made?"

"We remembered your friend Mr. Holman ran The Home Movie Company," Bert explained. "We went to see him, and he agreed to make it for us at school."

"So that's what you children were doing in the James Building!" Mr. Bobbsey exclaimed. "I wondered about that!"

"It must have been on the day you left me after our Christmas shopping trip!" Mrs. Bobbsey added.

The twins nodded vigorously.

"And we earned money to pay Mr. Holman!" Flossie cried.

"Yes," Freddie put in. "Nan and Flossie and I helped Aunt Sally Pry with her candy, and Bert shoveled walks!"

"That's where you went when you disappeared after school and on Saturday morning!" their mother observed. "I knew it must have something to do with your Christmas secret, but I couldn't imagine what!"

"You're very thoughtful children to do that," Mr. Bobbsey said, "and your mother and I appreciate your wonderful gift all the more because you worked for it."

At that moment on the screen, Nellie, as the old witch, shook her fist at the prince and princess.

"They won't do what she wants them to do," Flossie explained. "Watch! Something awful is going to happen!"

In the next scene the witch waves her wand over two figures completely covered with white.

"See," Freddie cried, "she's turning Bert and Nan into snow statues!"

"Very exciting!" Mr. Bobbsey commented.

"Do I recognize my sheets, Freddie?" Mrs. Bobbsey asked in an amused tone.

Freddie nodded.

"And I thought you were going to play ghost!" his mother exclaimed.

Flossie continued to describe the play. "The prince and princess can come back to life only if the witch waves her magic wand over them!"

"That magic wand," Dinah chuckled, "looks mighty like that old mop handle you got out of the basement, Flossie!"

The little girl giggled. "It is," she admitted, "but we sprayed shiny stuff all over it and it isn't a mop handle any more!"

"Flossie and I play very important parts now," Freddie announced proudly. "We're the younger prince and princess and we save Bert and Nan from the witch's spell!"

On the screen Flossie is dressed in a long pink skirt with a little silver jacket. On her head is a tiny crown of sparkling jewels. Freddie wears tight, black velvet knee pants and a red jacket. He, too, has a small crown.

"Miss Moore let us use the Council Room for our rehearsals," Nan explained.

"That was nice of her," Mrs. Bobbsey remarked.

"And you all look very royal!" Mr. Bobbsey added with a twinkle in his eyes.

At that moment in the movie Flossie seemed to be explaining something to Freddie as the little prince. The subtitle read:

A Plot is Formed!

"This is where we play a trick on the witch," Freddie said, his eyes dancing with mischief.

Freddie and Flossie creep through the doorway. Each holds a big balloon. Flossie, looking off in the distance as if she has just caught sight of someone, puts her finger to her lips, and the two children tiptoe inside.

"Here comes the witch," Freddie explained.

Nellie, in a long, tattered garment and leaning on a stick, totters onto the scene. She pauses in the middle of the screen and her body shakes as if she is cackling fiendishly.

"Now we play our trick," Flossie said, wriggling with anticipation.

The little prince and princess steal up behind

the witch, one on each side of her. Suddenly each one holds up a large pin and sticks it into his balloon.

The witch jumps up in the air and her magic wand drops to the ground! Quickly the little prince picks it up and the two children run off!

"They have the magic wand and can set us free," Bert said.

On the screen flashed the caption, ACT THREE.

"This is the last act," Nan said, as the gleaming snow castle was the center of the scene.

In the castle courtyard stand two motionless white figures. The little prince and princess enter and pause in front of the frozen pair. Then with both of them holding the wand they wave it over the heads of the still figures.

With a sudden motion the white robes are thrown aside and Bert and Nan as the prince and princess are revealed!

Mr. and Mrs. Bobbsey, Dinah, and Sam applauded heartily.

"The next scene is inside the palace," said Nan. "This scene was made in the big basement room in school."

There is a backdrop painted to resemble a hall lined with marble columns. In the foreground Bert and Nan are seated on white thrones.

"Looks like some of my cartons!" Sam chuckled.

"Yes, they're the ones we borrowed," Freddie admitted.

As the audience watches, Freddie and Flossie drag the witch into the room and set her down in front of the prince and princess.

A caption, "The Witch Is Banished!" flashes onto the screen. The last scene shows Nellie as the wicked witch walking sadly out of the room while Bert and Nan and Freddie and Flossie dance happily around the thrones.

As the picture ended, Mrs. Bobbsey threw her arms around Nan. "Your play is beautiful!" she cried. "And you children are wonderful to give us such an original Christmas present!"

"Yes indeed you are!" Mr. Bobbsey agree. "I propose three cheers for the Bobbsey twins!"

"We had a lot of fun doing it," Nan replied.

"And we had trouble too," Freddie added.

Then the children took turns telling their parents of various difficulties, especially with

Danny and how he had tried to spoil their plans.

"Danny's a prankster all right," said Mr. Bobbsey. The twins were to find this out in their next adventure, *The Circus Surprise*.

"Danny even threatened to tell you about our play," Bert said to his parents.

"But we kept our wonderful winter secret!" Flossie crowed in triumph. "Isn't it too bad that Christmas comes only once a year?"

Carol Malley
162 Sumner Ave
Springfield Mass.
7324458   01108

Holy Name School
Sister Alice
G.N.S. Rom. 13